She Say,
She Say

ISBN (softcover):   978-0-9852119-0-5
ISBN (e-book):   978-0-9852119-1-2

Printed in the United States of America

Cover Art by: Tiffany McPeak,
            Treating Your Smiles Like Fine Art Photography

Models: Sirius Wizdom
            Jacoby Beasley
            (For booking, contact at jacobybeasley@gmail.com.)

Editing and Interior Layout by:
            Carla M. Dean,
            U Can Mark My Word Editorial Services

Acknowledgements

To sit down and write a book takes a lot of discipline, love for the art of writing, and a lot of one-on-one time with your computer or pen and paper. It also takes having a support system to help you get through those times of writer's block, laziness, and wanting to throw in the towel.

I want to show love and gratitude to those who have been there to inspire me, brainstorm with me, critique me, motivate me, and do whatever else they could to help me make my dream of sharing my love of writing a reality.

First, I want to thank my mother, Jean Faulkner. Thank you for your constant support in ALL of my dreams. I love you, Mama! (Yes, I'm a mama's girl and proud of it!)

Shayla "Shh Be Still" Warren, had it not been for your forum this tale may have never been born, and I am so glad you've created a place to give others the platform to jumpstart their dreams, as well. Thank you.

Jacoby Beasley, Tiffany McPeak, and Sirius Wizdom, without you guys my cover would have been a pair of overused lips. You all made my characters real, and I am so grateful. I wish you all the greatest success in your own ventures. And Sirius...NO EXCUSES! ☺

Carla M. Dean, this has been a long time coming, and I am glad to say YOU are my editor. Thank you for your patience, your advice, and giving me a forum where I could actually learn about the industry. (I am *still* learning!) I wish you success beyond your wildest dreams. And hey, maybe I will be a member of the Artistic Words family soon! *Wink!*

Thomastrius Ladae Williams (yes, the gub'ment), I don't even know where to begin to let you know how much I appreciate you. I appreciate the foreword so much! You've got me feeling like I'm the shhhh! You've always kept it real with me (whether I liked it or not), and you've been an inspiration to me. We are now one for one on the books. It's time to get to work on those second ones! I love you bunches, Madam Iron Fist!

To my friends and family who have gotten sneak peeks of all of my writings, shared their thoughts, motivated me, and pushed me to keep going: Desiree, David (I'll pay you back when the book takes off!), Carra, Angie, Rico, Christal, Karen, Ki, Shammai, John, Shanay, Van Lisa, Monika, Kecha, Coby, Karen, Felicia, DeWonna, Shamikia, Cynthia, Larry, Lele, and a score of others—I am beyond grateful for your words, caring, and support. I share this accomplishment with all of you.

If I missed your name, know that it was because of my mind and definitely not my heart.

Thank you so much…

Dedications

First and foremost, I want to dedicate this book to the most magnificent woman that I know, Mrs. Ida Jean Faulkner. Mama, without you there would really be no me. You helped mold me into the woman that I have become, and I am so grateful. I thank you for always telling me to "Stick to it". I'm glad I listened in this case. Thank you for always having faith in me, as well as showing me how to be a strong, self-sufficient woman. No other woman compares to you. I love you.

I also dedicate this book to my baby girls, Devon and Dasia. You two are the air that I breathe. You are the reason I don't give up. You are my gifts from God. Mommy loves you.

Foreword

Congratulations! You have just embarked into one of the most anticipated literary voyages since the night before your best childhood Christmas! I sincerely hope you are ready to pause life for a few days while you addictively turn page after page of *She Say, She Say*. While this may be her first novel, Olivia Renee Wallace has been creating this masterpiece for quite some time. Her passion for the words you are about to read will not go unnoticed.

For some years, Wallace has teased minds with short stories. Her fan base captured the audience of hundreds of online bloggers and readers. Similar to a skilled painter, Wallace has nurtured her craft and love of writing, ultimately becoming one of the best erotic short story authors of our time. This book will read like fine art in a museum. *She Say, She Say* pulls you in, stirs emotions, invokes thoughts, and warms up the love below.

I have not only been a fan, but I also have had the pleasure of becoming friends with Wallace several years ago. Her determination is immeasurable, her will is unstoppable, and the heart that she has poured into this project will surely make you an instant fan. Knowing her personally, I can insure that these words come from a special place. One rule all writers abide by, "Write about things you know." When you write from a place of knowledge, your words have more meaning. The story is clearer and the personal connection is instant. Instead of words jumping off your page, the scenes play out in your head like a late-night cable channel movie.

Wallace provides all the ingredients of an instant bestseller with her two main characters, Shanelle and J.B. Their story is familiar to many who have dealt with new love, coming out, and dealing with life's many twist and turns. There are plenty of "OMG" moments to keep you on the edge of your seat. Wallac eloquently paints a picture of each character, as each woman tells the story from her own point of view. As these two women explore and develop their friendship, you can't help but to feel as if you've known J.B. and Shanelle. You can relate to their pain and sacrifice. The storyline will not only make you read it again, but you also will be highly anticipating her next book release (again).

I personally want to thank you for supporting this up and coming author, as well as my dear friend aka the Queen of 360 Erotica! Oh, and please spread the word:

Olivia Renee Wallace is here and ready to make your nighttime read just a bit sexier.

Thomastrius L. Williams
Author of *Too Real For Fiction: A Memoir*

She Say, She Say

BY

OLIVIA RENEE WALLACE

Chapter 1
Meet J.B.

J.B.

I caught her looking at me again, but for the life of me, I couldn't figure out why.

Shanelle Carter.

Miss Popularity is who she was – one of the most well-known females on campus. Half of her family was alumni, and even a dorm had been named after her grandfather. She was in her final year and about to get her Bachelor's Degree, a member of A.K.A., and a cheerleader. She had all sorts of volunteer work listed on her résumé. In everyone's eyes, she was a model student.

Fine as hell, her body was like that of a Goddess, with a nice booty and a pair of legs that had everybody in a constant state of awe. She had a face that was beyond pretty whether she wore make-up on or not. Skin the hue of warm honey. Beautiful lips and stunning almond-shaped eyes that changed from golden brown to nearly green, depending on her mood. Yeah, I admit I'd checked her out a few times, but who hadn't?

And as far as I knew, she was straight as hell.

She was dating this lame dude named Travis. He seemed like the kind of guy who was happier spending time in the library or coffee shop with her than taking her out to dinner and a movie.

She was nice, but in an uppity kind of way. You know, she was the "I'll speak to you and smile, but don't expect a long conversation" type of nice. I guess being born with a platinum spoon in their mouth would make one kind of uppity. She never really acted stuck up towards me, but then again, she never really paid me any mind either. And why would she?

She was a high-class good girl, and there I was – a big ol' studdin'-ass mofo. A sexy one, but an obviously gay mofo nonetheless. Imagine the controversy and all of the slack she would catch from her more stuck-up companions just from being in my presence. Heaven forbid!

But why on Earth did she keep looking at me? If I didn't know any better, I would've thought her straight ass was checking me out. I was sitting in the library listening to my MP3 player and going over some notes, when I felt someone watching me. Out of reflex, I looked up and saw her looking - or better yet - observing me from her table that was directly in front of mine. I half-expected her to look away quickly like she had done the first couple of times I caught her staring. Instead, she held my gaze for a minute before returning her attention to whatever she was working on.

I didn't know whether to be offended by the brief stare or turned on. I returned my attention back to working on my notes, but I felt it again and knew instinctively that she was looking at me again. This time, I didn't look up. I sat and debated for a moment on whether or not I would get up and see what the deal was with her.

Chapter 2
Meet Shanelle

Shanelle

Damn! She caught me looking again.

This time, I willed myself not to look away quickly because I didn't want to look foolish or like a shy schoolgirl. Although fascinated by her, I would have never expressed it aloud.

She was gay, and everyone in the world knew she was gay, whereas I had no idea of what I was. True, I played the dating game and never lacked male attention. After all, I was considered "Miss Popularity", and I was aware of that. Dates to formals, parties, and social events fell in my lap like leaves to the ground in the fall.

However, I had a secret that I had been carrying with me for a while. I had always noticed women, too. And I was very curious about her. I was curious about her before I even knew she was a woman.

Before anyone goes assuming anything, I will explain very quickly. My curiosity grew from reading her articles and editorials in the school paper.

J.B. Donovan was the name credited to the editorials that I found myself looking forward to every week, hot off the presses. I was curious to learn the identity of this individual who amused me and was so thought provoking. When I saw a picture of her in the paper and found out she was a woman, I was surprised to find myself attracted to her almost instantly.

I began seeing her at various places around campus and caught myself staring on more than one occasion, which had brought me to this moment. I found it hard to concentrate on my notes knowing she was sitting at the table in front of mine.

Her locs fell well past her shoulders and framed her cocoa-toned face as she looked down at her notes. Her head swayed slightly as she listened to something on her MP3 player. I must admit an innocent little fantasy that began with her glancing at me had started to unfold in my mind. Then suddenly, as if reading my mind, she looked up at me.

Those intense brown eyes pulled at me, and for a moment, I found myself drowning in them. Her eyebrow rose slightly, almost as if asking me a question. Unable to handle the gaze she returned for much longer, I looked back down and pretended to look over my notes while trying to normalize my breathing.

Silently, I wished I had the nerve to talk to her without worrying about what everyone else would have to say if they saw me approach her. I longed to be just a regular chick on campus, going unnoticed my most, instead of constantly being in the public eye where anyone from the faculty to my sorors kept me under a magnifying glass. More than anything, I wished she would approach me.

"Excuse me."

I looked up and there she stood, almost as if I had conjured up her closeness.

"Yes?" I said, managing to play it cool.

"I don't mean to bother you," she began, "but I've been doing research for the past three days, and I haven't had contact with another human being since I started. Would you mind if I sat with you for a minute or two just to break away from the books?"

I looked around and realized that, oddly enough, we were the only two people in the library.

"Sure" was all I could say. I tried to remain neutral, but inside, I was screaming.

Oh, how her voice caressed me. It was smooth, and she had an accent that made it obvious she was not from the south, but just a hint of a southern drawl had bled into her dialect. I felt the hairs on the back of my neck stand up. *Okay,* I thought to myself. *Keep it cool, girl.*

"Thank you," she said, taking the seat right in front of me. "So how are you, Ms. Carter?"

"Oh, you know me?" I asked, unable to stop a smile.

"Come on, girl," she said, returning a smile. "Who doesn't?"

I couldn't help but to laugh a bit. "I guess that's kinda true," I admitted.

Inwardly, I cringed and hoped I didn't sound too full of myself.

"I'm J.B.," she said.

"I know," I responded before I could catch myself.

"Oh really?" Her eyebrows rose in interest and surprise. "And just how do you know who I am?"

"Honestly, I'm a fan of your editorials in the paper," I answered, though I knew there was more to my awareness of who she was.

"Oh really?" she repeated, a grin spreading across her Carmex-protected lips. "That's very nice to know."

"You do good work," I told her, actually beginning to relax in her presence. "I can hardly wait until the next paper comes out tomorrow."

"You are so good for my ego," she said with a slight laugh.

"I'm glad I could help you with that," I told her, smiling.

I felt silly because this simple informal conversation with her had me smiling uncontrollably, even though we hadn't really said much.

"So is that why I keep catching you staring at me?" she asked, throwing me off guard completely. "Are you starstruck by me?"

As I sat speechless and trying to figure out how to respond to her query, I was saved by the P.A. system.

"The library will be closing in fifteen minutes. Please gather your final selections and..."

"I guess it's about time to round things up," I stated, grateful to change the subject.

"I guess so," she said, a thoughtful expression on her face. She rose from her chair as I rose from mine. "Thank you for the company, even though it was brief."

"It was my pleasure," I replied sincerely.

"I would love to continue this," she informed me.

When I looked at her and said nothing, she continued.

"Would I be overstepping my boundaries if I invited you out to lunch?"

My breath caught, and I knew she witnessed it. In my mind, I was screaming, *I want to BE your lunch*, but instead, I answered, "I don't know."

"Why not?" she challenged. "Are you afraid of what folks may say if they saw Miss Popularity with a big ol' stud?"

I felt my face get warm because she had hit the nail DIRECTLY on the head.

"Why would you think that?" I asked, not liking the look of slight disappointment in those mesmerizing eyes of hers.

She gave me a look that said, *Bitch, please*. After a moment, she sighed and said, "I'll tell you what. How about I give you my number, and if you aren't scared, you give me a call and let me know where you'd like to have lunch. Then I'll make it happen."

She reached into the back pocket of her Sean John jeans and pulled out a wallet. She then retrieved a business card and passed it to me. Our fingers grazed one another; the shock from the touch was unmistakable. My eyes flew to hers, and the look in them said she had felt it, too.

"Interesting," she said, almost to herself. She then spoke to me. "You have the number. The choice is yours, Miss Lady. You don't have to be afraid. I won't bite."

And with that comment, she stepped away, got her things from where she had been sitting prior to joining me, and walked away without looking back.

I didn't realize my hands were actually trembling until I looked down at the ivory business card in my hand. Why on Earth was my entire body humming from just the contact between our fingertips? I was pretty sure she was aware of my attraction for her. My reactions to her gave me away easily. Now she was daring me to step out of the "box" and have lunch with her.

I had to ask myself, *Do you have the nerve to do it, Shanelle?*

Chapter 3
The Phone Call

J.B.

She stayed on my mind constantly after our brief encounter at the library. I saw her in the library several times, but she was never alone. She was either with her friends or that lame guy she was dating.

Yes, I knew she had a guy. Did I care? Call me trifling, but no, I didn't care. If he had his thing together with his woman, she wouldn't have been eyeballing me all the time, and she definitely wouldn't have responded to a simple touch between us like she had.

But, I can't lie. I felt it, too.

Every now and then, I would catch her peeking at me, and I would just smile at her and shake my head. I knew she was curious about me, but she had this whole "image and reputation" thing going. Well, as beautiful and interesting as I thought her to be, I wasn't going to chase her. There were too many cute little femmes running around on campus who made it clear they had an interest in me. I had given Shanelle my number, and it was up to her to use it. I wasn't going to hold my breath while she debated on whether or not she was afraid to be seen with me for the sake of her image. However, I could give her something to think about.

Just over a week after our exchange, I shared my thoughts on images and reputations with everyone on campus through the editorial section she was such a big fan of. I could only imagine what she thought of it. I was out to dinner with a young lady named Lisa when I found out.

My cell phone played a snippet of Drake's hit "Over", signaling an incoming call. The waitress had just sat down a seafood sampler appetizer as I reached into my blazer to pull out my phone. Seeing an unfamiliar number, I let my date know I had to take the call because it might have been business, and I didn't turn down the opportunity to make some extra dough.

"J.B. Donovan," I answered in my business-like tone.

"I feel special knowing that you wrote an editorial just for me."

I recognized her voice immediately. I couldn't stop the smile that crept across my face.

"Well, well, well! Look who decided to drop me a call. What can I do for you tonight, ma'am?"

"You can quit trying to tempt me with your editorials," she answered. "I know what you're trying to do."

"Is that right?" I challenged, momentarily forgetting I was still out on a date. "And what exactly is that?"

"You're trying to get under my skin," she informed me.

"Is that right?" I repeated with a short laugh.

"Yes," she responded. "But, I'm not going to let you do it."

Is she trying to challenge me?

"Is that right?" I said again, feeling the smile growing even bigger on my face.

That's when Lisa cleared her throat to regain my attention. Remembering she sat across the table from me, I mouthed my apology and then returned my attention to Shanelle.

"What number is this?" I asked her.

"It's my cell," she answered.

"Okay. Well, I will give you a call back in a little while, okay?

Until then..."

Before she could say anything else, I pressed the end button on my phone and focused back on my date for the evening.

"I'm sorry about that," I told her before taking a sip of my White Zinfandel.

I can't lie; I rushed through the rest of my date with Lisa. We had already been to the movies, and I barely tasted my food as we made small talk. My mind was on Ms. Carter. When the waitress asked if we would be having dessert, I quickly informed her that I wouldn't be having any in hopes that Lisa would follow suit.

She didn't.

"I'll have a piece of the vanilla bean cheesecake, please," she told our server.

I wanted to groan in frustration, but I contained my impatience like a champ. When the cheesecake arrived, she wanted to have more idle chitchat while slowly eating her dessert.

"You know what?" I told her. "Your cheesecake is looking pretty good. Do you mind if I have a small bite?"

Thrilled that I wanted her to share with me, she happily put a nice-sized portion on her fork and held it out to me. I took it into my mouth and swallowed, barely tasting it at all.

She was so glad to share with me that she offered me another piece, then another. Before long, we had consumed the piece of dessert, and I was paying for the check. If I had waited on her to eat the damn thing by herself, it would've taken forever!

After leaving a tip on the table, I escorted Lisa to the car and took her home. I walked her to her door, gave her a kiss on the cheek, and thanked her for a nice evening. After watching her go inside, I made my way back to my black Camry, got inside, and immediately donned my Bluetooth earpiece. I called my last received number and waited for her to answer the phone.

"Hello."

"Hello, Ms. Carter. How are you?" I said, sounding as cocky as ever while starting up my car and putting it in drive.

"I'm mad at you," she answered. "It took everything in me not to call you back after you hung up on me."

"Why didn't you?" I challenged her. "Were you afraid it would be proof that I had gotten under your skin?"

"You think you're funny, don't you? Well, you're not," she said.

I could hear the humor in her voice, so I didn't take her comment seriously.

"I might be hilarious, but it seems you're afraid to find out," I responded, knowing that my words would eventually get her to say either yes or no.

"I'm not afraid of you," she debated with me.

"I never said you were," I stated simply. "I know it isn't me that you fear. It's everyone else that you're afraid of."

She said nothing.

"It's okay," I informed her. "I understand. But, are you going to go through life afraid of what someone else has to say? That's not a good way to go, girlie."

I gave her a moment to ponder on my statement.

"You could be missing out on a good friendship just because you're letting everyone else's opinion of you rule what you do," I continued. After another moment of nothing, I sighed, growing slightly impatient. "Well, it's plain to see that you are not ready to be your own woman yet, so call me when you are, okay? Goodnight, Ms. Carter."

Then I hung up.

I drove the rest of the way to my small apartment off campus in silence. I must admit I was disappointed by the fact that I wouldn't have the opportunity to get to know Shanelle, and even worse, that she was too afraid to take a chance at getting to know me. But, life goes on.

I made it to my apartment, went inside, and immediately took a shower. After throwing on a pair of black sweats, a sports bra, and a black wifebeater, I used a couple of my locs to secure the rest of my hair and the nape of my neck. Then I went into my living room and put on Chrisette Michele's *I Am* CD so I could relax a little bit. I retrieved a beer from my fridge and grabbed the latest edition of SOS Poetry. After taking in a few verses, I laid back and just let Chrisette's "If I Have My Way" soothe me.

Before I knew it, I had nodded off and there she was—hacking into my dreams. I saw myself kissing her. Touching her. Tasting her. Bending her over my couch. Making her moan.

I awakened, startled. Yes, she was fine, but I had never dreamed about her before. Not to mention, she passed up my invitation to lunch. Therefore, I considered it a done deal.

So why was I dreaming about dickin' her down somethin' serious?

I got up from my brown leather sofa, turned off my stereo, and made my way to the bedroom. I looked at the clock as I lay in the bed. It wasn't even eleven yet. I had cut my night short in hopes of making something happen with Shanelle.

My Drake ringtone rang out in my silent room. Considering the time of evening, I figured it could have only been a family member or one of my friends, so I answered the phone without looking at the caller ID.

"Yeah?" I said as a greeting.

"I can't let you make a punk out of me."

My body tightened in response to her voice. "Oh really?" I replied with more bravado than I felt. "It seems like you were doing a good enough job of that on your own," I told her.

"Are you going to try to make this hard for me?" she asked.

"Probably," I answered, putting my free hand behind my head as I found a comfortable position on my bed.

She sighed. "Fine," she said with mock exasperation. "I'm doing this just to show you that I'm not afraid."

"Is that your only reason?" I asked her. "Because if it is, you can save me the trouble—"

"No, it's not the only reason," she said, interrupting me.

"Well, what else is there?" I pushed. "You gotta give me something, woman!"

She laughed a little bit. "I find you interesting," she confessed. "I'm not giving you anything else until we have lunch, though."

"That's good enough for now," I said, unable to keep a pleased smile from coming onto my face. "When and where?"

"Well, I'm free this Saturday, which is a rare thing," she answered.

"Saturday it is." I was supposed to play ball with some friends, but that could definitely be put on hold. "Okay, now where do you want to go?"

After a few moments, she replied, "I don't know. How about you pick the spot?"

After thinking for a few minutes, I smiled to myself. "I know the perfect place. Will I be picking you up or would you like to meet me somewhere?"

Much to my surprise, she gave me the address to her apartment, which wasn't too far from mine.

"I'll pick you up at noon on Saturday then. Dress casual."

"I look forward to it," she said almost shyly, which I thought was cute.

"So do I," I told her before saying good night.

I lay in my bed, grinning from ear to ear.

She said yes, and I couldn't wait.

Chapter 4
The Date

Shanelle

Who are you really? Is your image keeping you from exploring new and foreign things? Is the way others see you keeping you from being YOURSELF? Can you step out of the small box that is 'Image' and be free to be the real you? I dare you.

She was talking to me.

No one else had a clue, but I knew she was speaking directly to me through her editorial column. I had no doubt about it. She was daring me to come to her.

So, I did.

It had taken all of three phone calls, but I did it. I got over my fear of calling her. So, there I was in my closet, looking for something casual, but eye-catching to wear on our date.

Date? Is it really a date?

I wasn't quite sure what to call it. An outing, I guess. But, if it was only an outing, why did I go through over half of my clothes in search of the perfect outfit?

I was still pondering over this when my cell phone rang. I looked at my caller ID and felt my pulse quicken when I saw J.B.'s name.

"Hello," I said, while thinking, *Do I sound breathless?*

"One more hour until you are seen in public with me," she said, almost as if taunting me. "Are you ready for that?"

"Why wouldn't I be?" I asked her as I lay across my bed like a schoolgirl.

"You tell me, Ms. Carter."

"There is nothing to tell," I debated.

Sure, I was a little nervous, but it wasn't so much about being seen with her. I was nervous because I would *be* with her.

"I will be looking for you in an hour. Don't be late."

"Oh, I'm very prompt," she assured me.

There was just a sliver of cockiness in her voice, and I liked it. She seemed so sure of herself.

"You just make sure you're ready for me," she added.

Was there a double meaning behind that comment? While my logical mind said, *Maybe, maybe not*, my awakened body screamed, *Please let there be!*

"I'll be ready," I told her before we said our goodbyes.

After stressing out over most of my wardrobe, I finally settled on a simple denim miniskirt, a red halter top, red sandals with wedged soles, and of course the appropriate accessories. I gently brushed back my freshly relaxed hair between my shoulder blades. It flowed easily because of the body wrap I had gotten just the day before. I went light on my make-up; a dash of eye shadow, a touch of mascara, lip liner, and gloss. I didn't want to make it look like I was trying too hard.

I looked at my reflection in my full-sized mirror and smiled at myself. Mission accomplished. Casual, but not bland.

I had gotten most of clothes back onto their hangers and into my closet when my doorbell rang. I checked my appearance again to make sure everything was in place before grabbing my purse and white Baby Phat jacket.

My hand trembled just a little bit as I reached for the doorknob. I opened the door with a smile and immediately took in her appearance.

She looked delicious in her attire, which consisted of caramel-colored khaki pants, a white oxford style shirt partially concealed by the caramel hued blazer that looked like it was tailor made for her. What gave the whole look a feel of being playful but GQ were the all-white S. Carter canvas-style tennis shoes that she wore on her feet. A black hair band held back her locs and diamond stud earrings twinkled like stars at her earlobes. However, not even the diamonds could compare to the smile that was on her face when I said hello. She was gorgeous!

"Are you ready, Ms. Carter?" she asked me.

"I certainly am, Ms. Donovan," I retorted.

I grabbed my keys from where they hung on my wall and joined J.B. on the small piece of concrete that pretended to be a porch in front of my door.

After locking my door, I turned to her and said, "I'm all yours."

She opened her mouth as if she was going to say something, but changed her mind. She had a smirk on her face as she led me to her black Toyota Camry. She unlocked and opened the door for me, then closed it behind me. I flicked the switch to unlock her door and then put on my seatbelt as I waited for her to get settled in her seat.

I felt myself relax almost instantly in the buttery soft seat. I took in the appearance of the car's interior. From the computerized monitor that sat where a stereo should've been to the stitched initials in the headrests, it was high-tech and, apparently, very personalized.

"Nice car," I told her as she started up the engine. "Were you selected on *Pimp My Ride* or something?"

"Nope," she answered, shifting the car into drive. "It was a guilt gift."

"A what?" I asked with a short laugh.

"A guilt gift," she said again. "When I first came out to my parents a couple of years ago, they were not very receptive. We went for months without speaking. Well, I came home for the Christmas holiday and lit into their asses over Christmas dinner, telling them to get over themselves because whether they approved of it or not, I was still their daughter and wasn't going to change. I made this big ol' grand exit and went out to my little Ford Tempo to leave, but the damn thing wouldn't start up for shit. So, I left it there and called a cab to take me all the way back over to my side of town. A week later, this car was parked in front of my apartment, and there was a note slid under my door that said if I accepted their apology, it was mine."

"So you accepted their apology?"

"We're riding, aren't we?" she said with a laugh. "There have been many other guilt gifts, and I'm going to keep taking them until they're tired of giving them."

"So are they buying your love?" I asked her.

"Hell no," she answered. "I love my parents no matter what. Everything they've given to me, I can get for myself. I don't have a problem earning everything that I have. But, it makes them feel better to give this stuff to me. Why deny them that?"

"I guess so," I said. "So what do your parents do for them to be able to buy you a pimped out Camry to win your affection again?"

"They're both doctors."

"Oh wow," I responded, nodding my head. "Impressive."

"Well, look who's talking," she said to me. "Half of your family owns the school."

"Come on now," I debated with a laugh. "That's an exaggeration."

We talked for so long that I didn't realize we had entered and passed by several towns on the interstate. As we continued to talk, our destination came into view.

The Ferris wheel couldn't be missed unless you were visually impaired. A country fair had been set up in a town that you passed through on your way to Anywhere Else, USA. There were no expensive paved parking lots. You parked on the grass or the dirt, and you didn't complain because it was free.

I could barely contain my excitement as J.B. put the car into park and turned the key to turn off the ignition.

"Ready to go play?" she asked with a devilish grin.

"Hell yeah," I answered enthusiastically, taking off my seatbelt.

I was out of the car before she could make it to my side to open the door. I hadn't been to a fair or carnival since I was in junior high school, so I was excited about going now. I was always too busy doing other things. I could only smile at her because of the place she had chosen to take me for 'lunch'.

After riding on the roller coaster, we decided to grab a bite to eat. As she ordered us a couple of corndogs, I got a glance at my appearance through a tinted window. My hair had been blown wild from the ride, and I became incredibly self-conscious about my appearance. I almost immediately started trying to groom my hair with my fingertips.

"What are you doing?" J.B. asked as she held two foot-long corndogs in one hand and one large drink in the other.

"Trying to fix my hair," I said, still trying to tame my wild mane as we made our way to a nearby bench. "I look a mess."

She passed the corndogs to me and sat the drink between us. In the gentlest touch that I could ever recall feeling, she brushed my hair and secured it behind my ear. As her fingertips grazed my ear, I felt heat flow from that ear to the rest of my body.

"You don't look a mess," she told me. "You look like you're having fun, and I mean the *real* shit. I'm guessing you don't do that enough."

"I just don't like looking crazy," I informed her, though for some reason, her light touch had me shaken to my core.

"Do you realize that you are beautiful?" she asked, her tone serious.

My breath caught in my throat.

"But even the beautiful don't have to look perfect all of the time," J.B. added.

She removed the band that secured her own hair, and her locs fell to her shoulders, framing her face. I wanted to touch them.

She stood up and walked around the bench to stand behind me. I sat as still as stone, unsure of what she was going to do. Then, I felt her fingers through my hair. Her touch was so soft that I nearly melted. She continued to stroke my hair with her fingers. She then took her hair band and wrapped it around my hair several times, making a well-secured, but comfortable ponytail. Her fingers brushed the back of my neck, and I wondered if she noticed the hairs that stood up at her caress.

"There," she said, sitting back down next to me. "Now you don't have to worry about your hair being everywhere." She then took her corndog and added a packet of mustard to it before taking a bite.

Normally, I wouldn't have ever been caught in public with a ponytail in my hair, but the way she looked at me at that moment made feel beyond beautiful. I felt my face get warm, and I couldn't look directly at her for several minutes. She had rendered me speechless, and her attention made me bashful.

Oh, this chick is good! To call her suave would not do her justice at all. How many guys had tried to woo me or run game on me? None of their attempts could compare to the simple moment that I had just shared with J.B.

Yeah, she was good.

After riding rides until neither of us could handle anymore, we decided to catch an early dinner at a nearby diner. We feasted on mammoth-sized burgers, fries, and shakes while talking about everything and nothing. I was enjoying learning more about her, and I found it easy to share myself with her. Honestly, I couldn't remember the last time I enjoyed myself so much.

Compared to all of the parties I've hosted or attended, I enjoyed the day I spent with J.B. much more.

Our 'lunch' turned into an all-day event, and I had absolutely no complaints. Shortly after nine-thirty, she was escorting me to my front door. It was dark on the front step, the streetlight being the only source of light since I hadn't thought to turn on my porch light.

I could feel her body heat as she stood behind me while I unlocked my door. I turned around to face her. She stood so close that I was able to catch a slight whiff of the Curve for Men cologne that she wore. I felt myself become slightly intoxicated from her nearness.

"Thank you for a wonderful time, J.B.," I finally said. "I had a blast."

"We could always do it again," she responded. Her voice had dropped an octave, and it was doing things to my senses.

"I think I would like that very much," I told her.

Had my voice changed also? Was that sultry sound coming from my vocal cords?

For a minute, we looked at one another in spite of the minimal lighting. Neither of us spoke. We just took each other in as if we were storing this moment in our memory. After clearing my throat as delicately as I possibly could, I broke the silence.

"Is this the part where I kiss your cheek and say goodnight?"

"Is that where you want to kiss me?" she challenged.

It was then that I noticed she was staring at my lips. She stepped closer to me, making my head swirl.

I felt her wrap one arm around my waist and pull me even closer to her. I thought I was going to die from anticipation. My heart started to race as she lightly brushed her lips against mine. I forgot to breathe as her tongue lightly drifted across my bottom lip, requesting access to my mouth. There was no way in hell that access would be denied.

I felt a slight moan work its way up my throat as her tongue caressed mine, coercing it to join hers in a sensual dance that I had never experienced with another woman.

Her tongue felt like satin against mine, her lips soft and slightly demanding. I felt myself being swept up into a whirlwind. She wrapped her other arm around me, and I found myself wrapping my arms around her neck, pulling her closer to my shorter frame. My fingertips played with her locs, which were as soft as I thought they would be.

She tasted of corndogs, Pepsi, cotton candy, and everything that was good in the world. I almost objected when she slowly and reluctantly pulled away from me.

My entire body was on fire from just her kiss. Before I even thought about it, I spoke.

"Would you like to come in?"

Chapter 5
Say Yes

J.B.

Damn, she looked so sexy right then. I don't think she was even aware of it. The diminutive bit of light from the streetlamp seemed to make her glow. Her lips were slightly swollen from our kiss. Damn, she tasted like heaven. The look in her eyes gave away the desire she was feeling for me. It turned me on and actually frightened me a little bit.

She invited me to come in. As much as I wanted to say yes, I knew if I followed her inside, I wouldn't be coming in for a cup of coffee and conversation. She knew it, too.

I wanted this woman...*badly*. I had tasted her lips, her mouth. Now I wanted to taste the rest of her. But, it was too soon.

"Would you like to come in?"

Her voice had become hoarse with her desire for me, and I can't lie, it was having an effect on me. However, I had to shake it off because I didn't want to rush anything or assume anything with her.

"I would love to," I informed her, "but I don't think I should."

Her face immediately fell. "I'm sorry," she said. Her head dropped slightly, and she averted her eyes from mine. "I didn't mean to seem like I was throwing myself at you or anything."

"I didn't take it that way. I just—"

"You don't have to explain," she said, interrupting me. She hastily backed into her front door, pushing it open with her butt. "I had a wonderful time. Thank you so much."

Before I could come up with something to say after bruising her ego, she quietly closed the front door on me. I heard her turn the lock, and for a moment, I actually felt guilty for doing the right thing.

I turned around and slowly walked down the steps and back to my car. Though I didn't turn around to look, I knew she was watching me through her window. I could feel it. Knowing *that* only made me want to go back up those steps, ring the doorbell, and give her what her eyes said she wanted. But, I had to maintain. Something about her made me want to take my time with her.

I quickly got in my car, started it up, and left before I changed my mind.

That night, I tossed and turned. My dreams were filled with her, and they were so real that I could taste her flesh and feel her hands touching my body. I awakened with my body drenched in sweat. I had joked with her about getting under her skin, but it seems the joke was on me, for she had gotten under mine instead.

The following Monday, I found myself in the library in hopes of seeing her and asking her how she was doing. I had tried to call her the day after our date, but she hadn't answered my calls.

I took a seat at my usual table, pulled out a few books and a notepad, and got to my busy task, while hoping to talk to her. True to her recent routine, she came into the library. However, she wasn't alone. She had the lame with her.

Was she trying to show me that she could be with whoever she wanted? If that was the case, she was doing a terrible job of it, because for the brief moment when our eyes met, her eyes spoke the truth. I saw the desire still in them, but there was something else.

For a second, I was stunned, because I then realized I hadn't just bruised her ego. I had actually hurt her feelings. I saw the pain mingling with the desire. Even as she looked away, I couldn't take my eyes off of her. I watched her sit with her boyfriend and pull out a few books and notebooks to start on her work.

It was easy to know when she was looking at me, because I hadn't stopped looking at her. I wished that lame-ass dude would leave so I could just have a few minutes to talk to her and clear up what she had mistaken for a rejection.

As if my silent prayer had been answered, his cell phone rang, and he walked away to take the call. I wasted no time getting up to make it over to her table.

"Shanelle—"

"Before you even say anything," she interrupted me, "I want to apologize for what happened Saturday night. I don't want you to think I just invite everyone into my home, because I don't."

"I never thought that you did," I assured her. "I just wanted to apologize for hurting your feelings. I had a reason for not coming in, and it had nothing to do with me not being attracted to you. If I had come in—"

"Shanelle, I have to go."

I looked up and saw her boyfriend approaching the table.

"My brother was in a car accident, and I have to get to the hospital."

"Are you serious?" she asked him in surprise, while getting up quickly to gather her belongings. She turned to me and said, "I gotta go. Sorry."

And they were both gone like the wind.

Damn.

I went back to my table, gathered my stuff, and headed home. My evening class had been cancelled, so I returned home. I got a beer from my fridge, turned on my PS3, and played video games until my phone rang. Looking at the caller ID, I saw it was my best friend, Jazz.

She was the only stud I knew who was cockier than even me, but she had a heart of gold that made it easy to see past her arrogance.

"Hey, what's up?"

"Not a damn thing," she replied. "What are you up to tonight?"

"Just chillin' around the house tonight," I answered. "Trying to figure out what to do about this lady."

"Oh? A new lady?" she queried. I could almost picture her ears going up in interest. "What's the deal?"

"She's feelin' me. I know that for a fact. And I'm feelin' her like crazy." I then began to tell her what was going on with her.

"From what I can see," Jazz began, "if she wants you and you want her, and y'all are two grown-ass people and know what you are getting into, I say go for it. I know you think you're a lil' player or whatever—"

"Come on now." I interrupted her with a laugh.

"Go to her," she continued as if I had said nothing. "Who is this apple of your eye anyway? Is she someone I know?"

I hesitated before answering. "Shanelle Carter."

"You bullshittin'!"

"Nope," I responded.

There was a moment of silence before Jazz spoke again.

"Damn! Really, really?"

"Really, really," I said back. "What do you think now?" I asked her.

"Personally, who she is doesn't change shit," she answered. "Go to her. Damn! Do you know how many mofos wanna tap that, and she just offered it to you on a platinum platter? You lucky bitch!"

I laughed. "Whatever, man," I replied, unable to stop the smile that came from my friend's comment. "I'm gonna holla back at you in a little bit. This stays between us, right?"

"You already know," she responded before disconnecting our call.

Go to her. That's what my partner in crime suggested. I know she wanted me, and maybe as bad as I wanted her, but would she accept me after I had hurt her feelings? I guess there was only one way to find out.

I picked up my cell phone and dialed her number. I silently prayed she would answer my call this time.

The Gay Gods must've been with me.

"Hello, J.B.," she said formally.

"Are you busy?" I asked.

"I just walked into my house," she answered. "Travis just dropped me off."

I immediately got up to grab my keys and my backpack that contained my...accessories.

"I'll call you back in just a minute," I told her, then disconnected the call before she could say anything else.

She was home without the lame, and I wasn't going to give her the opportunity to find a reason not to talk to me. I hurried to my car and drove the six blocks that separated her place from mine. With my bag thrown over my right shoulder, I went to her door and rang her doorbell.

She opened the door slowly. She looked sexy as hell in her oversized t-shirt. From the looks of it, that was all she had on. Nevertheless, she seemed completely comfortable standing at the door with it on.

"What are you doing here, J.B.?" she asked with an unsure look.

"I wanted to see you," I answered honestly. "Can I come in?"

She hesitated for a second before stepping aside to let me inside of her small, but nicely decorated living room. I walked across the ivory carpet to the black sectional sofa that dominated one corner of the room. I took a seat and looked at her, not saying anything. She tucked a strand of hair behind her ear and sat at the far end of the sofa.

After a moment of awkward silence, I asked, "How's your boyfriend's brother?"

For a brief moment, she looked confused and then said, "Oh! He's okay. He's a little banged up, but he will be fine."

"I'm glad to hear that."

More silence.

I looked at her from where I sat on her couch. She looked back, appearing to be unsure of what to say to me. I cleared my throat and sat my backpack on the floor next to my feet.

"What's in the backpack?" she asked, curious.

"Just some stuff," I answered quickly. "You never finished letting me explain what happened with me Saturday night," I began.

"There's nothing to explain," she retorted. "I got caught up in the moment and made a fool of myself. Simple. But, it won't happen again. I assure you."

"I know," I informed her. "But, I have to explain to you why I wouldn't come in."

She opened her mouth to speak, but I continued.

"If I had come in with you, I wouldn't have had any intention of leaving, and I wasn't prepared for that. I didn't want you to have anything to regret on Sunday morning."

"So what's so different now?" she asked, looking at me with those mesmerizing eyes.

"I'm better prepared," I answered. "And I'm willing to do whatever to make sure you won't regret it later."

Her eyes widened slightly as I eased closer to her on the sofa and spoke to her in quiet tones.

"If you want me to leave, I'll leave," I told her. "But, if you want me to stay, I want you to know I will be here until the sun rises. I won't be playing games when it comes to what I will do to you."

Seeing her bottom lip tremble, I couldn't resist running the pad of my thumb across it as I touched her face, drawing her closer to me.

"So what'll it be?"

I felt her breath on my lips just before she closed the small distance between us. This time, her tongue invaded my mouth, and I happily allowed the entry. I could taste the hint of mint toothpaste on her tongue. She was as delicious to my senses as she had been on Saturday night. I pulled her closer to me as I felt her fingers playing with the dreads at the nape of my neck.

Damn, this woman kisses like a dream!

Before I realized I had even moved, I pulled her onto my lap, and she straddled my waist. My hands easily found their way under her oversized shirt, and to my delight, she was indeed naked underneath. I groaned into her mouth at my discovery, my hands roaming over her silky back. She moaned as I ran my hands over the ass that I had only fantasized about touching. I felt her shiver when I played with her nipples, making them stand at attention.

I had to feel the rest of her.

I wrapped one arm around her waist to make sure she remained well balanced upon my lap. Then, with my free hand, I slowly made my way to the heat that was emanating from her center. She whimpered into my mouth upon the initial contact of my fingers to the center of her womanhood.

Lord, help me. She's so damn wet.

She moaned, shook, and whimpered as I began to slowly stroke her deep within her wetness. It wasn't long before she came.

"J.B.!" she called out against my lips. She rocked her hips against my fingers, unable to stop trembling the entire time.

"Don't fight it, baby," I groaned as her juices flowed over my fingers and hand.

"I w-wouldn't know how to," she stammered while holding me

tightly. "Oh my Gawd, J.B.," she moaned in wonder.

"Yes, baby girl," I mumbled into the crook of her neck. I was so turned on, but I was nowhere near finished with her yet.

"We have to stop," she said in a hurry.

"What?" I said, looking at her from where she remained on my lap. "Why?"

I knew I may have sounded crazy, but by then, I didn't care.

"I have to be completely honest with you before we can continue this," she said, looking down at me, her breathing still uneven.

I waited silently for her to continue. She looked nervous, which made me nervous, too. What she said next nearly pulled the rug from under me.

"I'm a virgin."

Chapter 6
Intimacy

Shanelle

I had to tell her...

As hot and bothered as she had me, I couldn't *not* tell her.

For a second, she just looked at me. "Excuse me?" she said after a long moment.

"I'm a virgin," I repeated, this time a little more loudly.

She lifted me from where I straddled her waist and sat me next to her. In spite of the turn of direction the moment had taken, I was still able to marvel at her strength and how easily she lifted and moved me.

"I don't understand," she said, looking at me. "How is that possible?"

"Well," I began, "when a woman decides at a young age that she will not have sex until—"

"I know what it means to be a virgin," she said, interrupting my babbling. "How could you still be a virgin? You're one of the most popular and beautiful women on campus."

"Does that mean I'm supposed to be givin' it up?" I asked, teasing her despite the seriousness of the situation.

"I didn't mean it like that," she sputtered. "I just don't understand *how*."

Her voice trailed off as she looked at me. She then shook her head in disbelief. I watched quietly as she settled into some secret thought of her own.

I was nervous to say the least. If she rejected me, I didn't know how I would take it. I was almost reduced to acting like a child when I invited her in and she turned me down before.

"Why me?" she asked suddenly.

"Pardon me?" I responded.

"Do you realize what you are offering me is a gift? This is something that, in a perfect world, should be saved for somebody you're in love with."

"Well, I hate to tell you this," I said quietly. "It's not a perfect world. And I have the right to give it to whoever I want to give it to."

"But why me?" she asked again. "I know you're not in love with me, so what gives?"

"I dunno," I answered. I thought for a minute before answering again. "Since the day I found out who you were, I've been curious about you."

"So you just want to appease a curiosity?" she asked, while looking at the floor. "I don't want to be your experiment."

"You're not letting me finish," I told her. "Since I've actually met you, you've been on my mind constantly. I'm not just curious about you anymore. I want to *know* you. If it were just curiosity, it could've ended the day you took me to the fair. Instead, I wanted to know even more about you. You've made me smile more than anyone else has in a while. I loved being in your company. You made me feel so nice, and it was genuine. I can't think of anyone else who I would rather give myself to right now."

She sat quietly for a minute, soaking in everything I had said. I hadn't meant to give her a speech, but I wanted her to know how I felt. I wanted to get to know her. I wanted *her*.

"What about your boyfriend?" she then asked. "How's he going to feel about you giving away your preciousness?"

"I don't have one," I answered with a short laugh.

I knew she thought Travis was my boyfriend. Everyone did. It kept most guys away.

"I thought—"

"I know what you thought," I interrupted. "He and I went out a couple of times, but decided very quickly that we would be better friends than anything else. I'm actually closer to him than most of the girls that I associate with."

She released her breath, apparently relieved by what I had just told her. I gave her major brownie points for having some moral issues with this, even if it were only a few.

Mustering up a little bit of nerve, I inched closer to her and touched her face. "There is something going on between us," I said to her, nearly whispering. "I know you feel it, too. Don't you want to find out what it is?"

"What if it just turns out to be a physical thing?" she asked.

It was then that it occurred to me that she was afraid, maybe almost as afraid as I was. Did she want us to have something going on?

"Then we'll know in the morning," I responded.

I don't know where I had scraped up all of this nerve to express myself to her. I just knew if I couldn't have anything else from her, I wanted this night.

Seconds seemed like hours as she stared at me. *Will she spend the night with me? Or has my honesty scared her into running away?* I silently prayed it would be the former.

"Are you sure you want this?" she asked me. "Once I get started, I won't be able to stop. I'm warning you now."

"Will you be gentle with me?" I asked coyly.

"As gentle as I can be," she answered, her voice dropping to that octave that made my body so aware.

I began to throb at my center with just the thought of what was about to take place.

"Then I am surer of this than anything I've ever been sure of before."

She then stood up from my sofa and reached for my hand. Though nervous, I wasted no time placing my hand in hers. She pulled me to my feet and spoke.

"Take me to your bedroom."

I led the way to my room with my heart going at what seemed like a thousand beats per minute. It beat so loudly in my own ears that I could've sworn she could hear it, too.

We entered my dark room, where I turned on the small lamp next to my bed. It casted a soft glow across the room, making it easier to see without being too bright.

I turned away from the lamp and found myself in her embrace. She wrapped her arms around me, pulling me closer to her. I felt safe in her arms as I wrapped my arms around the back of her neck, meeting her halfway to share a kiss that nearly made my knees buckle. As our tongues danced seductively with one another, I reveled in the feel of her hands on my body.

My head fell back when her lips moved from mine. I moaned lightly as I felt her tongue traveling against my jugular vein before she gently nipped me on my shoulder. I whimpered in objection when she pulled away from me. Then, to my surprise and pleasure, she reached for the hem of my t-shirt and pulled the garment over my head.

I stood before her completely naked. As she stood back and looked at my body, I grew warmer under her gaze. I thanked my lucky stars that I had shaved and trimmed up everything while I was in the shower. The look of desire in her eyes made me feel more beautiful than I had ever felt. I felt like she was worshipping me with her eyes.

She reached out and ran one finger over my body. Her finger trailed from my lips to my neck. She then made lazy circles around my areolas, causing my nipples to harden like little diamonds. Next, she ran her finger down my belly, lightly playing with the piercing in my navel before trailing further down to where my body yearned for her presence.

She slid two fingers between the lips that protected my womanhood. I moaned and gripped her shoulders.

"J.B., please," I begged, nearly crying out.

"Relax, baby girl," she whispered in my ear. "I've got you."

She kissed me again before picking me up, which shocked the hell out of me, and placing me in the center of my queen-sized bed. She almost immediately placed her head at my right breast. Her tongue circled my hardened nipple before she gently took it into her mouth. My back arched in reflex as she lapped at my breast before switching to the other. Her hands roamed over my body and her mouth followed. She touched and kissed me everywhere from my lips to my feet. I had never expected the feelings to be so intense as she caressed me with her hands and mouth.

My body didn't seem to whet her appetite; she wanted to devour my soul, as well. I realized this once she parted my thighs and made herself comfortable between them. I looked down to see her face so close, her lips so close. I watched in fascination as her tongue eased from between her lips to part my flesh below. My eyes rolled back, and I closed them tightly when I felt her tongue graze my clitoris lightly for the first time.

"Mmm..."

The moan escaped before I could stop it. My fingers found their way into her dreads while I pulled her further into my femininity. I writhed beneath her as her tongue massaged my clitoris teasingly at first and then with more force.

"J.B.!" I called out. "Oh shit...baby!"

She groaned with pleasure. "Are you ready to cum for me?" she asked against my wetness.

Not waiting for my response, she returned her attention to my throbbing puss, stroking me mercilessly with her tongue. I felt like I was on fire. I was going to explode if she didn't stop. But, I would die if she did. Never before had I felt anything like how she was making me feel.

"J.B.!" I called out again.

Her name had become a song, and I couldn't stop singing it. I gripped her dreads tightly, holding on to her for dear life as my orgasm hit me so hard that I thought I saw stars and flashes of light.

"Yes," she said triumphantly into the pussy I had already decided belonged to her.

She devoured me. She drained the life force out of me. The very essence of me now flowed from my body into her mouth and throughout her system. With just her mouth and her touch, she had possessed me.

After giving me a few moments to recover, she came up and lay beside me.

"Are you okay?" she asked quietly.

"I am wonderful," I answered, still breathless.

"You taste so damn good," she said brazenly. "I can't wait to have some more of you."

My clit jumped at her comment.

"But, there is more I plan to do to you tonight."

And with that, she gave me a quick kiss on my lips, causing me to have a small taste of myself. She then rose from the bed and left the room.

I closed my eyes and relaxed in spite of her departure. I couldn't recall ever feeling so at ease before. I hadn't even realized I had dozed off for a minute until I felt her warmth next to me. She had taken off some of her clothing and turned off the lamp. Only the faintest light came into the bedroom from the living room.

My eyes adjusted to the darkness, and I turned to face her.

"Are you ready?" she asked me.

I didn't have to wonder about what she was referring to. Our time had come. I could only nod now. My nervousness had returned, and it was a natural thing. I was about to give her my virginity. I was allowing her access to a place no one had ever been before. I was terrified, but I wanted this.

She positioned herself above me, between my legs. Sensing my nervousness, she spoke again.

"I will take care of you," she pledged, and I believed her. She adjusted herself and positioned her phallus at the gateway of my womanhood. "Let me know when it's too much for you," she instructed quietly.

I nodded in understanding, still speechless about what was about to come. My body stiffened a little bit as she began to push herself into my moistened pot. At first, my body resisted.

"Relax," she coerced gently. "You're in good hands, baby girl."

Slowly, I began to relax. After a few moments, I felt the head enter my body.

"Oooh," I moaned as she slowly entered me, stretching me, pushing past a barrier that had never been touched before. My nails dug into her shoulders as an exquisite pain shot throughout my entire being. "Mmmm," I cried out as she gradually withdrew from me.

"Should I stop?" she asked.

Even in the barely lit room, I could see the mixture of concern and desire in her deep, dark eyes.

"No," I answered. "I want this."

Needing no other words, she eased backed into my wetness, giving me slow and shallow thrusts so I could adjust to her size. I moaned and released sighs as my pain became pleasure. Her shallow strokes went deeper, and I called out her name in bliss as she made love to me.

She pulled my legs around her waist, driving even further inside. It hurt and felt good at the same time. I didn't want her to quit. I begged her not to stop.

"You got me, baby," she told me, breathing hard while fighting to keep her desires in check to make sure my first time was as memorable as possible.

She was turning me out. I admit it. As she dug deeper and marked my pussy as hers, I knew I was hooked. She had me. I was so far gone. She had me floating on a cloud of bliss. I knew I was going to fall in love with her. It was just a matter of time.

She stroked me and kissed me gently. The touches grew more intense as the time went by. My orgasm hit me with such a fury that I cried in her arms. I had never felt anything like it. She cooed and soothed me as I shook in her embrace. She adjusted me so I could lay my head on her chest.

"How do you feel?" she asked while stroking my sweat-dampened hair.

"Sore," I answered honestly. "But, it's a good thing. Will it always be this good?"

"We can definitely work on keeping it that way," she replied.

"I would like that," I informed her as I threw one of my legs over hers.

After a few moments of comfortable silence, she asked, "What do you want from me?"

After a minute of thinking, I answered, "Whatever you are willing to give."

More comfortable silence.

"What if I catch feelings for you and I want you to be my lady?" she then asked. "How would that work? I know who you are, and I know how I am. I wouldn't want to be a secret."

I thought about it for a while. Just a short while ago, I was worried about what people would say if they saw us together. I knew it was on her mind, too.

"I don't know," I answered truthfully.

Would I be strong enough to handle all of the bullshit that would come my way once everyone caught wind of my relationship with J.B.? I wasn't sure, but as good as she made me feel, both in the bedroom and out of it, I knew in my heart I was determined to try.

So, I told her, "This is new ground for me, but I'm willing to try whatever it takes to find out where this can lead to."

"Well, that's a start," she said after a moment. "I'll take that for now."

"So does this mean you might end up wanting me to be your lady?" I asked her shyly.

"Maybe," she answered. "We'll talk more about it in the morning. We still have work to do. I am nowhere near done with you yet."

"Is that right?" I challenged, unable to hide my smile.

I didn't know how much my body could take so soon, but once she pulled me to her for another one of those delectable kisses, it looked like I was about to find out.

Chapter 7
Falling

J.B.

I had to have her again. Though I was the dominant one, her gentle caresses overpowered me. She was just so sweet. I tasted her again, drank from her again, and got lost in her again. I couldn't resist.

She felt so damn good. Her skin was silky and hot against mine, even as her body was lightly covered with perspiration from our lovemaking.

Her lips were fuller from the tons of kisses we exchanged. Her face bore no make-up, just the lightest layer of moisture. Her hair was damp, some plastered to her forehead...wild. And she looked like a woman satiated.

She was beautiful.

My heart slammed into my chest when I looked down at her face. She had nodded off with her head upon my chest.

She scared the hell out of me. As I felt her deep, slow breathing and felt her heartbeat against my skin, I realized how dangerous she was. *I could fall in love with this woman.* The realization of that little fact made me want to jump out of her bed and run home to hide.

I'd only been in love once before, and it didn't go too well. I knew it was too soon to even be considering the possibility, but I also knew love had no timetable. Hell, my parents met when they were young and married after only three months of dating. Twenty-plus years later, they were still in love. Was it possible for something like that to happen for me?

I shook my head to try to clear it. Nelle nuzzled up closer to me. I had already started thinking of her as 'My Nelle'. I thought about what my homie, Jazz, had said. There were a ton of folks who would give a body organ for this woman, and she chose me. I smiled to myself. That had to mean something, right?

As I pulled her closer to me, she made a noise that sounded almost like a purr. She wasn't just beautiful. She was adorable.

Damn it, man!

I could feel it coming...

I was falling...hard and fast.

This wasn't supposed to happen like this. I thought a night together would at least ease my longing for her. However, finding out that she was a virgin and wanted to give her virginity to me made me only want her more. The way she moaned and called my name, the way she responded to me, and how she sounded when she came, only increased my desire for her. I could really feel her wrapped around me. I felt every stroke. Her nails in my skin only made me want to please her more. *Damn.* She made me wish I had been born with a dick.

It took all of my willpower to keep a reign on my own desires to make sure she would be able to cherish our first night together. Oh, my Gawd! Hearing her call out my name like that made me feel like I was on top of the world. No one would ever be able to say my name and get the same response that she pulled out of me. She had a hold on me, and she didn't even know it.

And I couldn't let her know it either. At least, not yet. It was way too soon for her to know the way she affected me. Don't get me wrong. I had no intentions of trying to be distant or hard towards her. I just couldn't give away any more than she already knew.

Eventually, I dozed off with her, loving how she felt in my arms.

*****

The sun came too soon. I had a class that I couldn't miss. She looked like an angel as she slept tangled in her sheets. I had showered in her bathroom, and she never stirred. I knew I had tired her out, so I wasn't going to bother her. She needed her rest. She took her first night of making love like a champ. I knew her body would be sore, because before the night was over, she took all of me, which was more than a lot for a beginner's body. She gave as much as she received, and I liked that shit. She was an awesome lover. I found it hard to believe a virgin could be so passionate.

It was almost like she was made for me. I shook my head while watching her sleep. I tried not to read too much into everything about the night before, but I couldn't help it. I couldn't describe how this woman made me feel so quickly. I vowed right then to take my time with her. I *had* to.

I leaned over her and kissed her softly on the temple.

"J.B.," she murmured, still asleep. I loved my name on her lips. "Baby?" she said in her sleepy haze.

"Get some rest," I whispered in her ear. "I'll see you tonight, okay?"

She opened one eye and smiled at me sleepily. "Okay," she said demurely.

How could one so sexy be so damn cute, as well? She fell back to sleep as quickly as she had temporarily awakened.

I grabbed my backpack and made my way to the front door. After locking her bottom lock, I gently closed the door behind me and made my way to the car. The sun shined beautifully as I drove the short distance home. Everything seemed brighter for some reason.

As much as I was trying to fight it, I knew it was a losing battle. I was falling for her.

Chapter 8
The Morning After

Shanelle

My thighs were sore and my body ached as I sat up in my bed.

I was in such a peaceful state, until my doorbell kept chiming in my ear. Thinking that maybe J.B. had left something, I eased out of bed and slipped on the shirt I had worn the night before. I took slow and careful steps to the front door and opened it only slightly just in case it wasn't J.B.

To my disappointment, it wasn't her.

"Girl, what are you still doing in bed?"

I looked into the face of one of my closest associates, Deniece.

"What time is it?" I asked, stepping out of the way to let her in.

"Almost ten," she answered, strutting into the living room. "When you missed class this morning, I decided I should probably check on you because you haven't missed a class in who knows how long. Are you sick or something?"

I was coming down with something, but it definitely wasn't an illness.

"I'm just really drained," I replied with an apologetic smile. "I think I just need to take the day off. I don't have any exams or anything major today. I just need to rest."

"Rest?" Deniece said, looking at me as if I had grown another head. She walked over to me and placed her hand on my forehead.

"What are you doing?" I asked, swatting her hand away.

"Checking for a fever," she answered. "You must be sick. You never take a day off."

"Well, there's a first time for everything," I told her, while taking careful steps over to my couch to take a seat.

I decided to lie on the sofa instead. I grabbed the remote control to my television and pressed the power button. I half listened to Deniece as she spouted the latest gossip about various people at our school, her new clothes, her car, and blah blah blah. My mind was really elsewhere.

The night before, I had experienced something out of this world. I had made love with JB. I sighed to myself as I recalled the events of the night before. My eyes drifted closed, and Deniece's voice faded into the distance as I remembered every kiss I shared with J.B. I could vividly see the desire in her eyes as she looked down at me. I felt every caress of her hands and lips all over again. I began to ache for her. I barely caught the moan that was working its way from my throat as I remembered that Deniece was still in the room with me.

As I watched Deniece continue to gossip, completely unaware that I was paying her no real attention, my body tingled with the memories of J.B.'s touch. Even though I had just lost my virginity the night before, I knew she was an exquisite lover. She was so gentle, making sure I was comfortable. She had made the night all about me. It was beautiful. We made love twice, both sessions wonderful. She kissed me...*there*...until I could take no more. Then she held me and caressed me until I fell asleep. It was better than any romance novel I had ever read.

It was real, and it happened to me.

"Shanelle, are you listening to me?"

I looked at Deniece and almost felt guilty for missing every word she had said. "I'm sorry," I told her. "I zoned out."

"I see!" she said, looking at me for a second. "What's got you all spacey this morning? Or is it a who?"

I was dying to share my previous night with someone, but I knew Deniece was not very good about keeping her mouth shut, so I simply replied, "Nunya."

She giggled with delight. "So it *is* a who!" she said, almost gleefully. "Come on. Spill it!"

"I'm not ready to share yet."

I lay back against my throw pillow and closed my eyes again, knowing she wasn't going to let the topic go that easily.

For a few moments, she said nothing. However, just as I suspected, she began her interrogation.

"Is it Travis?"

"No."

"Is it...um..." She thought for a minute, snapping her fingers as if it would help her conjure up the correct name. "Is it Fernando, that cute Kappa? Ya know, the mixed guy?"

"No."

"Oh! Is it John, that Omega?"

"Hell no!" I answered, my eyes popping open at the absurdity of her query. "He is such a man-whore! Not even close!" I couldn't help but laugh.

"Well, who is it?" she asked, dying to know.

"You'd never guess," I told her as I sat back up on the sofa. "Girl, I'm tired. I'm about to go and lay back down in my bed."

"Is that your way of putting me out?" she asked, though she already knew. She rose from her seat and grabbed her purse.

"Yes," I answered honestly with a chuckle, while standing up, also.

"Fine. Be that way," she said with an exaggerated pout.

"Make sure you call me tonight," I told her. "We still have to meet with the other girls so we can finish getting things together for the fundraiser anyway. I'm still riding with you."

"Okay." She stepped out of the front door and on to my small porch. Then she turned around and looked at me. "So you're not going to tell me who it is?"

"Nope," I responded with a cheesy grin as I closed the door in her face.

"Fine then, poopie head!" she yelled from the other side of the door.

Deniece was a very sweet chick and very funny. If she weren't such a gossiper, she would probably be my best friend. But, I would hate to have to kill her for blabbing my personal business.

I laughed as I made my way back into my bedroom. I wanted to take a shower, but my legs were still kind of wobbly. So I opted to lie back down.

My thoughts returned to J.B. and our night together. I actually felt my heart start beating faster at the images that popped into my mind. I could hardly wait until my body wasn't so sore. I wanted her again at that very moment. I hoped I wasn't going to turn into some sex-craving nymphomaniac. She just made me feel so good that I wanted more. She was so skillful at the art of making love, making me feel like I was floating on a cloud. She had become my drug. I was addicted.

When she kissed me goodbye, I wanted to ask her to stay, but I was so tired that I could barely say anything at all.

Intelligent, fun, gentle, and an awesome lover. She was just what I needed in my life.

I could feel the smile on my face even as I dozed off.

*****

I awakened to the sound of my cell phone ringing. I smiled when I looked at the display and saw her name flashing on the little screen.

"Good morning," I answered, still a little sleepy.

"Morning?" she said. "It's almost three o'clock, beautiful."

"Really?"

"Yes," she replied. "Did I wear you out like that?"

I could hear the humor in her voice.

"Oh, don't go getting big-headed," I warned her, unable to stop smiling.

"I'm not," she responded. "But, I must've done something right. I put you to sleep. You were snorin' and stuff."

"I was not!" I said, unable to stop the laugh that flowed from my soul.

She knew how to make me laugh, and I loved it. Suddenly feeling a little shy, I spoke quietly.

"Thank you for staying with me last night."

There was a very short silence before she responded. "I wouldn't have wanted it any other way, baby girl. Thank you for letting me stay."

My heart skipped a beat at the tone of her voice. "When will I see you again?" I asked, hoping I didn't seem too anxious, but in all honesty, I was.

"When would you like to see me again?" she inquired.

"As soon as you want to see me," I answered.

"Then come and open your front door."

"You're here?" I asked, unable to hide the excitement that had trickled into my voice almost immediately.

I sat up quickly and climbed out of bed.

"Mm hmm," she answered.

"I'll be right there."

I disconnected the call and headed for the front door. I caught a glimpse of my reflection and quickly ran a brush through my hair in an attempt to tame it a little bit. I then rushed to the door as quickly as my legs would take me.

I didn't care anymore that I seemed anxious as I threw the door open. There she stood looking as gorgeous as ever, holding a single red rose.

"Hi," I said meekly.

"Hello," she said, flashing those pearly whites in my direction as she handed me the rose. "Did you miss me today?"

"Maybe," I responded with a grin, then sniffed the beautiful flower and stepped aside to let her in.

I closed the door and turned around to find myself in her embrace. She leaned forward to kiss me, but I immediately turned my head and covered my mouth.

"I gotta brush my teeth," I told her from beneath my palm.

She laughed and stepped back. "Well, hurry then. I want those lips."

My body immediately grew warm.

"Awww," she said. "Look at the baby blushing!"

I shoved her lightly as I made my way to the bathroom, where I quickly brushed my teeth and gargled with a little mouthwash. I then grabbed a face towel and washed my face, closing my eyes as the warm towel soothed my skin. When I opened them, she was standing there looking at me through the mirror. The look in her eyes was unmistakable.

"I want you again," she said quietly as we made eye contact via the mirror.

I immediately began to throb at my center because of those four simple words. I couldn't speak for a minute. I could only look at her, enchanted by her. I opened my mouth to speak, but nothing came out.

She walked up to me and wrapped her arms around me from behind. She then placed the softest of kisses upon my neck.

"We have plenty of time," she whispered into my ear. Even her warm breath on my skin was a caress. "Right now," she continued, "I want you to go into your living room, turn on the television, and relax. Okay?"

"Okay," was all I could say as she escorted me back into my

living room.

She watched me as I lay on my sofa and grabbed the remote. After flashing a smile, she disappeared back into my bedroom. I could only imagine what she was up to, but I couldn't wait to find out.

Chapter 9
Her Secret

J.B.

She had been on my mind all day. I could barely focus on my work. I missed her even though we had only been apart a few hours.

Damn. I wasn't ready to feel like this. I asked myself over and over if I was moving too fast with her. I didn't want us to be too hot, too fast and then fizzle out.

I'd seen it happen over and over again amongst us lesbians; falling in love after a few conversations and kisses. Then being ready to move in together after one or two good lovemaking sessions, only to find out a month or two later that they barely even like the person who was "wifey material" a few short weeks before.

I didn't want Nelle and me to fall under that lesbian stereotype. Then I thought about it. Was Nelle even a lesbian, or was she another straight woman who was fascinated with the idea of being with me? Not that I'm being cocky, but I've had my share of "straight" or "undercover" women. Would Shanelle be just another one? Or could she be my ride or die chick?

These questions began to vanish from my mind once I heard her voice over the phone. They were almost completely non-existent when I saw the smile on her face when she opened her door to let me in.

She was adorable. I laughed as she rushed away to brush her teeth so I could kiss her. As I stood and watched her from the bathroom door, I could speak what was on my mind.

"I want you again."

I sensed her body's reaction. It was almost like our bodies were connected without even touching.

I regained control of my libido and shooed her into the living room so I could run her a bubble bath. As she soaked away the remaining soreness from our previous night together, I straightened up her bed so I could give her a massage with the scented oil I had brought with me.

I went into her bathroom to check on her and found her laying with her head back, seemingly at total ease with the world. I went and got a cup from her kitchen before returning to the bathroom.

Kneeling beside her tub, I whispered in her ear, "Relaxed?"

"Very," she said with a smile, never opening her eyes.

"Good," I responded before proceeding to wash her hair.

I love how she stayed relaxed and trusted me with her body and hair as I cleansed her from head to toe. After helping her out of the tub, I dried her off and escorted her to the bed, where I massaged her body from her temples to her toes. Though I tried my best to keep a reign on my desires, I could not resist tasting her until she screamed my name over and over.

I was addicted to the very taste of her. I loved how her wetness flowed over my tongue and into my system. I couldn't get enough as she pulled me deeper into her wetness, tangling her fingers in my locs as I consumed every ounce of her sweetness.

As she lay in the bed recovering from her afternoon "massage", I called and ordered Chinese food as an early dinner. Shortly thereafter, we were relaxing on her living room floor while eating and watching a movie.

Her hair was pulled back into a ponytail, clean and conditioned from my shampooing. She wore a pair of gray sweatpants and a white tank top with her Greek letters blazing across the front of it. Not a single drop of makeup touched her skin, and she couldn't have looked more beautiful to me.

"What?" she asked with a slight smile.

"Nothing," I replied. "I didn't mean to stare. You're just so beautiful."

I saw her blush before she shyly looked down into her paper container filled with shrimp fried rice. "Thank you," she said demurely, unable to look me in the eyes for a moment.

I couldn't resist reaching out to her. I took the container out of her hand and put it on the coffee table. The food was immediately forgotten as I kissed her slowly, lowering her onto her back on the soft carpet.

She wrapped her arms around the back of my neck and spread her legs so I could lie comfortably between them. For moments, we just enjoyed kissing each other. I hadn't planned to touch her at all, but I couldn't resist.

This woman had the craziest effect on me. I couldn't seem to get enough of her. When I finally found the strength to try to pull away from her, she moaned in objection and wrapped her legs around my waist, causing me to almost completely lose my already weakened control. As I moved to kiss her on her neck, I heard her moan my name. I can't deny it; it made my pussy jump.

"Damn, girl," I whispered against her neck in awe of her effect on me. "You turn me the fuck on!"

My breathing had already become labored. I continued to struggle with my libido, determined not to let this delicious woman ruin my self-control. However, as she slowly began to roll her pelvis upward against mine, I knew I was going to lose the fight.

As if it had a mind of its own, my hand snaked its way into the waistband of her sweats and immediately dove between those lips that I wanted to kiss so badly. She was already wet and ready for me. I felt myself start to ache as I slowly began stroking her, gently playing with her clitoris and then sliding two fingers deep into her wetness.

"J.B.!" she called out. "Baby!"

"You like it, baby girl?" I asked.

She could only moan and nod as I continued to service her with my fingers.

"Tell me when you're about to cum," I commanded as I thrust my fingers in and out of her, letting my thumb massage her pearl.

I felt her small nub grow harder beneath my thumb, and I already knew before she even screamed my name that she was about to get hers.

"J.B., I'm about to—"

"I know, baby," I whispered with a harsh breath. "Just enjoy it."

I think I enjoyed it as much as she did. I felt her womanhood constrict around my fingers as she came all over my hand. She trembled and gripped my shoulders for dear life, moaning loudly. She was uninhibited as she rode my fingers, and I loved every moment of it.

I was addicted to her.

We both lay on the floor saying nothing afterwards. She laid her head on my chest while taking her time coming down from her high. I closed my eyes and enjoyed the feel of her body against mine. I could've easily fallen asleep, but the ringing of her cell phone interrupted our solace.

"I don't wanna get it," she said lethargically.

"It might be important," I told her.

I reached onto the coffee table, grabbed the annoying cell phone, and passed it to her. I really didn't want her to answer it either, but I wanted to be considerate.

Still lying on my chest, she answered the phone. "Hello? ... Hey, Deniece. What's up?"

She then shot straight up.

"Oh damn! I forgot."

I watched as she quickly rose from the floor. As she continued her conversation, she motioned for me to get up from the floor, too.

"Where are you? Who's with you?" I heard her ask. "Okay. I'll see you in a few."

She then turned her attention back to me. "That was my friend Deniece," she explained to me quickly. "She will be here in about fifteen minutes to pick me up. I forgot we had a meeting tonight about our fundraiser, and I said I would ride with her."

"So let me guess," I began. "You need me to dip."

Her face immediately fell, and I felt bad for it. I knew it was all new to her, but I already felt myself wanting more with her, and I knew already I did not want to be a secret.

"Please don't be mad at me," she said, her eyes instantly sad in spite of the pleasure I had just given her. "I'm just not ready to expose this part of myself to my girls yet."

The word "yet" caught my attention and gave me a little hope. So, I shook off my negative attitude and walked up to her.

"I'm not trippin', baby girl," I told her as I wrapped my hands around her small waist. I gave her a soft kiss on her lips. "Go get yourself ready. I will put the food up and see myself out."

"Are you sure?" she asked, still looking unsettled.

"Yeah, baby," I assured her, kissing her one more time.

I smacked her playfully on the butt and nudged her towards her room before cleaning up our half-eaten food. By the time I put the food in the refrigerator, she had already selected an outfit and was in her bathroom getting ready to do a rush job on her hair with the flat iron.

I kissed her on the neck, and she turned around to hug me real tight. She smiled and thanked me for being so understanding.

"No big deal, baby," I guaranteed her. "I got you."

I grabbed my things and walked out of her front door. As I

backed out of the parking space, I asked myself if I was prepared, mentally and emotional, to be her secret.

Chapter 10
Fears Addressed

Shanelle

I didn't want her to leave, but I wasn't ready to present her to my friends yet. Honestly, I didn't know when I would be ready. I knew how much I was enjoying the time we spent together, but I still had an image to uphold.

My image. That is what had started all of this.

I mean, if I let the world know that J.B. and I were an item, wouldn't I still be the same Shanelle Carter? Wouldn't I still be an A.K.A.? Wouldn't I still be the same woman who got involved in tons of community projects? Wouldn't my academic record still exist? I had no doubt all of these things.

What scared me is how people would start to perceive me? Would they start to think I was nasty, promiscuous, or against everything traditional? Would the members of my church consider me an abomination? How would my family view me if I told them that I was in love with another woman?

In love with her?

I admit I was already falling head over heels for J.B. But, was love enough?

Was I strong enough to accept the odd and sometimes nasty looks we would get if we were seen holding hands in public?

Would I be able to kiss her in public and not care what others may be thinking about us? Would I be able to hold my head high when an ex-boyfriend sees me with her and calls us a couple of dykes?

I wasn't sure.

I had never been involved in a situation like this before. This was foreign territory to me, and it scared me half to death.

What I did know is how my heart raced when she kissed me, how my skin felt like it was on fire when she touched me, and how she gave me butterflies with just a look. And I genuinely enjoyed our time together! I could just relax and be free with her. I needed that. Deep down, I felt like I needed *her*.

So why was I so terrified?

Chapter 11
Between Friends

J.B.

Why was I so pissed off? I mean, I knew this whole thing was new for her. And I tried to be understanding, but damn!

I wanted her to be my lady. I wanted to learn about all of her ups and downs, ins and outs. I wanted to take her on dates, do things with her, have portraits done and shit. Meet her family. Introduce her to mine. We couldn't do any of that as long as I was her secret.

I didn't want to have to rush off from her place whenever her friends called and said they were coming over. I never had to deal with this undercover shit with a woman. I'd never been in a real relationship with a "straight" woman, so I never had to dip because she didn't want her secret discovered. This whole thing was already starting to bother me. But, damn it! I had already fallen for her. This woman had my mind blown. I had already become attached.

After sitting in my quiet house for an hour, I grabbed a beer from my fridge and called up Jazz.

"Sup, pahtna," she said as a greeting without preamble.

I told her, "I done went and fucked up."

"How?" she inquired with a chuckle. "What did you do now?"

"Me and Shanelle—"

Olivia Renee Wallace

"Y'all boned?" she asked excitedly, interrupting me.

"Yeah," I answered while nestling myself into a more comfortable position on my loveseat. "We did."

"Awww shit now!" she exclaimed. "Details! And don't leave nothin' out!"

Normally, I wouldn't have a problem sharing my sexual escapades with my best friend, but for the first time ever, I wanted to keep it between me and my lady.

"Not right now," I told Jazz.

"Ain't that some shit?" she said, her disappointment evident in her voice. "So what else is there to this story?"

She knew me so well.

"I think I'm in love with her."

She immediately started laughing. "What the fuck, yo?" she said. "Stop playin'." After a few minutes of my silence, she sobered from her giggle-fest. "Are you serious, J?"

"Yeah, man," I confided. "No bullshittin'."

"Damn," she said after a pause. "Are you sure about that? I mean, it hasn't even been that long."

"Yeah, I'm pretty positive about it," I responded. "She's got my mind blown."

"Damn," she repeated. After almost a minute of total silence, she spoke. "The pussy's that good?"

Unable to stop a laugh from springing from my throat, I corrected my homie. "You are nuts. It's not even about the sex, Jazz. It's *her*. Her smile, the way she blushes when I stare at her, her intelligence, the way she smells…"

"You *are* in love, huh?" she responded, amazement in her voice. "You're saying all of this soft shit and soundin' all poetic and shit. Look at how the mighty player has fallen."

"Oh, shut the fuck up," I said with a laugh. "I just don't know what to do about it."

"What are you talking about?" Jazz wanted to know.

72

"She got this whole persona bullshit going on," I explained. "As far as the world knows, she's straight. Hell, and we both know I'm far from it. Right now, we're doing this secretive shit, and I don't like this shit at all."

"So what are you gonna do about it?"

"I don't know," I answered, my frustration seeping into my voice. "I'm not used to being anybody's secret. I'm not afraid or ashamed of who and what I am. But, I'm trying to understand her situation, too. I know this is all new to her and she's afraid."

"What could she possibly be afraid of?" Jazz demanded.

"Everything and everybody," I answered. "I can understand, because in the beginning, it wasn't easy when I first came out to my parents. At the same time, though, I don't know how long I will be able to do this like this. I mean, I had to leave her place because her friends were on the way over. It was almost like she was ashamed to be seen with me, and you know I'm not going to be able to keep my cool with that shit."

"I feel you on that," Jazz agreed. "You still haven't said what you're gonna do about it."

"That's because I don't know what I'm gonna do about it," I confessed. "I've never been so messed up about a woman, and so fast!"

"Since it's happened so fast," Jazz began, "how do you know it's real?"

"Because," I answered, "I've never felt this way before. Not even with Nita, and you know how crazy I was about her."

That was the first time in a long time that I had even brought up my ex, my first real love. Nita and I had been together for a couple of years. Yet, my feelings for Nita couldn't hold a candle to how I was already feeling for Nelle.

"Damn," Jazz said, almost in awe. "That is crucial, man. You and Nita were the 'it' couple for a long time."

"I know, right?" I agreed.

For a moment, neither of us spoke, both lost in our personal thoughts.

"So you feel more for this girl than you felt for Nita?" she asked.

"Yes," I answered.

"But, you were ready to wife-up Nita until all the bullshit went down," she addressed.

"I know," I responded, taking a swig of my beer.

"Damn, pahtna," Jazz said after a moment. "I don't know what to tell you. You done fucked around and fell for a closet chick."

"I know!" I exclaimed, unsure of how I felt about it.

My best friend's voice was filled with amusement when she made her next statement. "You know you're about to catch hell with this one, right?"

After taking another sip of my beer, I responded, "I'm pretty sure of it."

All I could do was hope in the end she would be worth it.

Chapter 12
Can't Blame Her

Shanelle

I wanted to make it up to her.

Even though she had said everything was cool, I still felt her becoming distant with me. It had been a week since we had spent any time together, and our conversations on the phone were always short. The fact that we hadn't seen each other, not even in the library, bothered me.

Was she so mad at me that she felt like she had to avoid me? Was there something more to it? Had she met someone who, unlike me, wasn't "in the closet"?

I knew her freedom to be herself was a big issue for her, and the fact that I still had to hide our relationship was a problem.

Our relationship?

Were we actually in a relationship? Did I even have the right to feel some kind of way because we hadn't spent any time together? We had never made any declarations about what we really were or whether or not we were even *anything* at all. At this point, I hadn't even gotten the nerve to tell her how much I felt for her.

It was way too soon to even whisper that I was in love with her. I wasn't trying to come off as some sprung chick that got turned out by another chick. I didn't want her to think I was tripping because she had given me some good lovin'.

And, my oh my, it was soooo good. In the week I hadn't seen her, I found myself craving her touch and her kiss. I spent several nights getting to know my body better as I envisioned the things she did to bring me pleasure.

Even more than her touch, I missed her smile, how she made me laugh and feel, and her company. I missed her. My days seemed bland without her.

As I sat in my living room eating from a small box of shrimp fried rice and watching *Imitation of Life*, I felt so lonely for her, but because of my stubbornness, I refused to call her again because I didn't want another short, impersonal conversation from her.

I didn't know what to do with myself. I wanted her, but I didn't want to risk being rejected. My feelings were even more involved now, and I was sure any kind of rejection would really hurt. I wasn't ready for that, so I did what any normal woman would do.

I called someone else.

"Hey, Shanelle," the voice said from the other end of the phone. "What are you up to, Miss Lady?"

"Bored," I answered. "What are you getting into tonight?"

"I was thinking about catching a movie. Nothing major, though. What's up?"

"Want some company?" I asked. "I got cabin fever."

"Sure!"

After getting details about the time and location, I finished my fried rice and made myself more presentable. Thirty minutes later, I was standing at the marquee watching as Travis paid for both his ticket and mine.

"Thanks," I told him, smiling as we walked towards the concession stand.

"No problem," he replied. "Thank you for the company. We haven't been out in a while, so this is nice."

"I agree. I apologize if I've seemed distant lately. I just got a lot on my plate right now."

"I understand," he responded. "I know how that goes. Trust me. I'm just glad to know you haven't forgotten about me."

He smiled and gave me a playful wink. I couldn't help but to smile back.

"Never that," I assured him with a quick laugh.

After getting a bag of popcorn, a pack of Twizzlers, and two drinks, we headed into the theater. After finding seats near the center of the stadium-seat styled room, we got comfortable and watched the advertisements and trivia questions that showed on the massive screen before the lights went out for the movie.

A few minutes before the lights dimmed, my eyes grew wide at the sight that unfolded before me. Coming up the steps with a gorgeous brown-skinned model-type chick was J.B.

The surprise in my eyes quickly transitioned to hurt and then anger as our eyes collided. The odd thing was her eyes did the same.

She paused for the briefest moment before stepping aside and letting her escort slide into a seat several rows directly in front of Travis and me.

I secretly fumed, and she looked at me with a humorless half-grin before shaking her head a little bit and sitting down next to her date.

So it's like that, huh?

As the room darkened, so did my mood.

I was so pissed that I couldn't pay an ounce of attention to the movie. I excused myself from my companion, telling him that I needed to use the bathroom before nearly stomping down the stairs. After going into the bathroom, I went into a stall and handled my business, pulling way too much tissue from the roll in my frustration. I sent a silent prayer that I didn't clog up the toilet as it automatically flushed once I stood up. I didn't even look back as I threw the door open to go and wash my hands.

Leaning against the wall, with her arms crossed over her chest, was J.B.

My heart raced, but I did everything I could to look oblivious to her presence. I washed my hands silently before walking over to the electric hand dryer. As the warm wind stream blew on my hands, I stood with my stiff back to her. After my hands were dry, I prepared for my grand exit, but before I could walk past her, her hand snaked out and grabbed my wrist.

I paused and looked at her.

"You not gonna say nothin'?" she asked, her irritation apparent.

"What is there to say?" I replied, my annoyance shining just as brightly.

"So you're not gonna explain to me why you're here with that lame-ass nigga?" she demanded.

"I didn't realize I had to explain anything to you," I threw back at her. "Why are you worried about it anyway? You're not exactly here by yourself!"

"She's my cousin!" J.B. hissed at me.

"Oh, come on!" I exclaimed. "That is so played out. I know you can do better than that shit."

Just as the restroom door opened, I tore my wrist from her grasp and made my way towards the door.

I ignored the curious looks from the two women who came in as J.B. called my name. I continued to head back into the theater. Instead of sitting back down, I told Travis that my stomach was bothering me. I told him to enjoy the movie and apologized for the wasted ten dollars before excusing myself.

"Do you need me to drive you home?" he asked, taking his attention away from the screen.

"I'll be fine," I assured him. "I can handle the drive. I'm just not feeling too hot."

He looked at me for a minute, causing me to feel uneasy about his penetrating stare. "Are you sure you're okay?" he asked. "I promise that I am okay," I told him, averting my gaze a bit. "I will text you when I get home so you know I'm okay." "Don't forget," he nearly demanded. I nodded before making my way out of the theater. I was so thankful that I had driven to meet him there, because I wouldn't have been in the mood for the small talk or the "what's the matter" questioning that I knew would come if we had ridden together.

During the drive home, my anger ebbed and slowly returned to hurt as I thought about how pretty J.B.'s companion was. Though I was still mad at J.B., I truly couldn't blame her.

Chapter 13
A Thin Line

J.B.

I'm not even trying to front. I was pissed off. I wanted to yank Nelle's ass up from where she sat with that lame-ass dude. I wanted to lay his ass out just for being there with her! I didn't appreciate seeing *my* woman at the movies with a dude, whether they were just friends or not. He was too close, and they looked too comfortable with each other. I didn't care about how long they had known each other. That shit was not sitting well with me at all.

After confronting her in the bathroom, I was even more pissed. She had gotten the last word in, basically calling me a liar, and then left me in the bathroom looking dumb as hell without the opportunity to explain myself. I knew that I came at her kinda fast, but I didn't care. She was my woman, and I was not cool with her 'friendship' with Travis. Yes, I was claiming my territory.

And I was pissed the fuck off at my territory.

I could barely focus on the movie after I regained my composure and returned to my seat. It bothered me to see she was not sitting in her seat, but at least I knew she wasn't with Travis, because he was still in his. After a few minutes, I came to the realization that she was not coming back. I completely lost interest in the movie and forgot that my cousin Khadijah was sitting next to me. I pulled out my phone and texted Nelle.

Where r u?

After ten minutes of not getting a response, I texted her again.

Don't igg me.

Five minutes passed before she finally responded.

Enjoy ur DATE!

Now that I knew she was okay, I became irritated with her attitude.

She's my cuzn!

GO 2 HELL! was her reply.

Damn. Was she really that mad? I didn't give a damn. She was going to talk to me. I stood up and motioned for my cousin to do the same.

"What are we doing?" she asked, confused.

"I gotta go," I responded with no further explanation.

After seeing the expression on my face, she knew better than to question me.

As we made our way to my car, she said, "You owe me a movie."

"I got you," I informed her.

As I pulled out of the parking lot, I felt sorta bad for cutting my cousin's night short. I would make it up to her in the future, but I had some business to handle with Nelle. I wasn't going to let her sit by and trip on me for nothing.

The drive to my aunt's house was a quiet one. My cousin jumped out of the car as soon as it came to a complete stop. Before she closed the passenger door, she looked at me and reminded me that I owed her. Then she added, "Don't get in any trouble, cuzzo. I know you."

"I won't," I promised her.

I watched her walk into the house before I pulled off to head to Shanelle's house. I had to let Ms. Carter know a few things.

As I drove to her place, all I could think was she better have had her ass at home.

*****

Once I got to her place, I sat in my car for a minute to try to calm my nerves. But, the more I pictured her in the movies with that dude, the madder I got.

I knew she was awake, because her porch light and her living room light were on. So, it pissed me off even more when I knocked on the door and she didn't answer. I didn't have time for these games.

I knocked again. She turned her porch light off.

Seriously?

I started beating on the door then.

"Leave me alone, J.B.!" she yelled from inside the house.

I beat harder on the door. "Open the door, Shanelle! Quit playin' and shit!"

"Go home or back to your date!" she yelled back.

As I continued to beat on the door, a neighbor's porch light came on.

"Don't make me act silly out here," I warned her. "Your neighbors are already starting to look."

That must have caught her attention, because she opened the door.

"Stop yelling," she said, though she wasn't exactly being quiet. "You're bothering my neighbors."

To my surprise, she let me in.

"You just don't want any of them to see you arguing with your girlfriend," I snidely stated while walking past her.

After closing the door, she crossed her arms over her chest. "Girlfriend?" she snorted. "I didn't realize I had one."

It stung, but I mentally waved it off. "Whatever," was my diluted response. "You know what it is."

"No," she retorted, "I don't. How can you sit there and be pissed at me for catching a movie with a friend, when I've barely heard from you at all lately? I've never been in a relationship with a woman before, but I have a little experience with relationships in general, and I know that when you ignore your boo, it usually means you don't want them anymore."

"I haven't been iggin' you," I argued. "We talk."

"We haven't had a conversation longer than two minutes in the past week," she said, annoyance evident in her voice. "And the first time I see you, you're with another woman!"

"She's my cousin—"

"I don't want to hear that shit," she interrupted. "That shit went out in high school. Please, do better."

"Well, what's up with you and ol' boy?" I demanded. "It didn't look like you were missing me too much!"

"Because you've been iggin' me!" she argued back. "I shouldn't have to miss you so much when you're only ten minutes away from me! You avoided me, so I called somebody who wasn't!"

"I don't want my woman cruisin' around with another muthafucka, and that's all there is to that shit!" I yelled.

For a minute, she just looked at me speechless. I tried to calm my demeanor as I watched her walk past me and into her bedroom. A moment later, I followed her path.

She leaned against her dresser and just stared at me with her arms crossed protectively over her chest. Even mad, she looked beautiful to me. And she had some fire about her, too. My baby wasn't a pushover. I was actually proud of that. I wanted a strong woman by my side. But did she even want to be there anymore?

"Look," I said, sitting on the edge of her bed. "I didn't like seeing you with him."

"Well, what am I supposed to do when you won't come see me or even talk to me?" she challenged quietly. "I'm not the kind to just sit idly by. I'm not trying to sound conceited, but you *do* know who I am. I've spent the past week or so waiting and hoping for some time and attention from you. I've never had to do that before. And then when I finally see you, you're with another woman. Do you think I enjoyed seeing that shit?"

For a minute, I couldn't speak. Truthfully, I knew I had been putting her off. I was finding it more and more difficult to be her secret. I wanted to be free with her, and I wanted her to be proud and free to be with me. The logical part of me understood it was still new to her. I really did! Still, the emotional part of me was selfish and wanted things to be exactly how I wanted them to be. I looked at her for a moment before quietly responding.

"I apologize for what it looked like, but she really is my cousin. Let me ask you a question. How do you think I feel to be your secret? I always end up feeling some kind of way when I have to disappear for your friends' sake."

Her shoulders dropped, and for a brief moment, I thought I saw defeat. But then, she squared her shoulders again, walked over to where I stood, and looked me in the eye.

"I know it's not easy," she answered. "I'm trying to get it together, but honestly, I'm afraid of the repercussions that may be involved with being open about our relationship."

I started to speak, but she interrupted me. "I'm just being honest. All I'm asking is that you try to bear with me for a little while longer and see things from my point of view. You have years of experience *being you,* and I am still trying to figure out who I am."

She stood there, and all I could do was think about how beautiful she was as she tried to look brave in front of me. I knew she was just as unbalanced about us as I was. I wanted it to work with us, but did I have the patience? As I raised my hands to lightly grab her waist, I figured I could at least *try.*

"Who you are," I began, "is a woman who has my head all

fucked up."

She draped her arms over my shoulders and asked, "Is that a good thing or a bad thing?"

I answered honestly. "I don't know yet."

Damn, she smelled so good. I wanted to touch her, but didn't want to rush. And just my luck, I had left my backpack at home. All the anger and frustration that had come from this night of misunderstandings dissipated and transformed into pure unadulterated lust. I pulled her closer to me and nuzzled her covered breasts with my lips.

"I missed you," I confessed against her body.

"I missed you, too," she admitted before bringing her petal-soft lips to mine.

Before I could pull her closer to me, I was gone. I drowned in the pleasure of feeling her tongue against mine. I was instantly drunk with desire for her. This woman was my crack, my cocaine, my heroine. She weakened my resolve. I craved her. I missed her. I wanted to taste her. I wanted to bury myself deep inside of her.

Since I couldn't do one, I would definitely do the other!

She didn't resist when I undid the button and zipper of her Baby Phat jeans. As the denim nearly melted from her round hips, my mouth almost watered in anticipation of what was to come. Before I could even think about removing her shirt, I slid my fingers beneath the flimsy material of her panties. She was already wet and ready for me. She whimpered as I slid my fingers between her moist lips. Her whimpers turned to moans as I slowly stroked her clitoris.

I then slipped two fingers inside of her cave. Feeling her buckle slightly, I held her tighter. I love how she gripped my shoulders as if she was trying to maintain her sanity. I continued to stroke her deep within her womanhood, alternating from her insides to her clit. She writhed and moaned as I continued my manipulation of her femininity. As I dipped my fingers in her honey pot, I felt her clit harden beneath my thumb.

"J.B.!" she called out while burying her face into my neck.

"Just get it, baby," I instructed, fighting my own desire.

My pussy started throbbing because of our interaction. I would definitely need some release later. I couldn't remember the last time, if ever, a woman turned me on so much. To know I was her first was an even bigger turn on. My mark was on that kitty; it was mine.

"Damn," I groaned as that fact really hit me.

It sent me on a new high. I needed her confirmation.

"Is this my pussy?" I asked as my fingers plunged in and out of her wetness.

"Yes!" she moaned loudly, gripping my shoulders.

"Is it really, baby?"

"Yes!" she screamed as my finger-work became faster and more intense.

"Tell me it's mine," I demanded, playing with her soaked clit.

I heard her scream, "It's yours!" as my fingers rapidly slid back and forth across her stiff clit.

"J.B., please!" she begged weakly, aching for her release.

I knew she was about to come. So, I pulled away and watched the mixture of surprise, confusion, anxiousness, and pleasure on her face. I was enjoying the sense of power that I had over her in the moment. I knew she ached for my touch, but I ached for her very essence. I slowly finished undressing her, letting my fingertips brush her warm skin. Her neck, arms, stomach, and thighs all seemed to grow warmer with my touch. Her nipples stood at attention, begging to be acknowledged by my mouth. My mouth *did* water at the notion that I would soon take each peak inside it.

I laid her on her stomach and placed kisses on the back of her neck before leading my tongue down her spine until I reached the curve where her juicy ass began. She moaned in excitement and anticipation.

Growing hot myself. I removed my shirt, leaving on my wife beater. I felt a bead of sweat run down my back as I looked at the silky, ready, naked body before me. She was perfect, and she was *mine*.

I raised her body until she was on all fours. Then I pushed her head and shoulders into the bed, making her back arch, which caused her to position her ass further into the air. I heard her sharp intake of breath as I spread her lips and slowly started licking her clitoris from behind. Her wetness spilled onto my tongue, and I drank in every drop. Her essence became a part of me as I lost myself in the sweetness of her nectar. I sucked her clit into my mouth and assaulted it with my tongue. She screamed out my name over and over again. I loved how she threw that ass back at me while I fucked her with my tongue.

I felt her body convulse as she came in my mouth. She tried to run, but I overpowered her, holding her in place. She fell flat onto her stomach, but I kept that pussy raised enough to continue my attack. She writhed uncontrollably, grasping at sheets as wave after wave of pleasure flowed from her body into my mouth. I was intoxicated; I didn't want to let her go. She tasted like heaven, and it had been too long since I had her.

I turned her over onto her back and immediately took her lips with mine. I knew she could taste herself in my mouth, but she kissed me as deeply as I kissed her. I knew she had missed me, too. I wrapped my arms around her as she wrapped her legs around my waist and began to gyrate beneath me, getting her moisture on the front of my white beater. *Damn. Why did I have to leave my backpack at home? I want to blow her damn back out!* I rocked against her in the traditional motion, wishing I could be inside her.

She continued to grind against me until she caught another nut. She moaned into my mouth, and my pussy jumped. I moaned helplessly into her mouth in return. This woman drove me to insanity. I wanted to touch my damn self!

I felt her hands move to the belt of my pants. She quickly freed it from the buckle before working her way to the button and zipper of my jeans. She worked quickly and deftly in spite of the closeness of our bodies. She grabbed my pants and underwear and pulled them down as far as she could. She then used her feet to finish the job. I was surprised, but curious to see where this newfound aggression would lead to.

Though I am a dom, an alpha-stud, I am also secure in the fact that I am still and always will be a woman. However, I admit the moan that came from my throat when she touched me was so feminine that I almost had to look around to make sure it came from me.

She purred as she turned the tables on me. I found myself grinding against her fingers as she rubbed me slowly, sending me closer to the edge.

"I want to please you," she whispered against my lips.

"Baby, you are," I promised her, while trying to "man up" and fight the torrent of sensations that she was sending over my body.

In a burst of strength that caught me off guard, she rolled us over until she positioned herself above me. She began to gradually grind her wetness against me, setting every nerve at my center on fire. She kissed my lips before moving to my neck. She paused to gently suck along my jugular before moving down to raise my shirt. The muscles in my stomach convulsed as she ran her tongue around my shallow navel.

My entire body tensed as she paused along my pelvis to sample the sensitive skin there. How had she known one of my weak spots? I reveled in the sensation as she manipulated my body like she had been doing it for a lifetime.

The pleasure that shot threw me when I felt her warm mouth embrace my womanhood was indescribable . I moaned in surprise and sinful delectation as she swirled my clitoris in her mouth. I was unprepared for the skill and confidence that she displayed while licking and consuming more than my damn pussy. She was eating me alive, devouring my soul, possessing me as only I had done to her. *Who was this woman?*

My shy Nelle had turned into my captor, making a soft bitch out of me with her mouth. If I hadn't known any better, I would've thought she was as experienced as I was. Who was the master? Who was the apprentice? It no longer mattered as I felt myself fall over the edge. Wave after blissful wave washed over me while she drank from me as though she had been deprived of food and water for days.

I couldn't control my convulsions and moans as she flicked her tongue over my sensitive nub over and over again before sucking on it with gentle force. I think my eyes watered a little at the pleasure she was giving me.

"Shit, Ma," I called out as another nut snuck up on me. "Damn!"

She gripped me as I had gripped her to keep her from getting away. I didn't know how to handle being the prey instead of the predator. I'm not going to act like I don't like getting head, but this was different. It was deeper. It was like she was absorbing me, making me a part of her.

She came to me and kissed my lips, and for the first time, I tasted myself on her tongue. I was drunk from the feel, taste, and touch of her.

I was so gone over this woman. *Damn.*

She nuzzled up to me and laid her head on my chest while still straddling me.

"You are something else," I whispered to her as I worked to regain my breath and composure.

"Is that good or bad?" she asked, looking up at me.

"Wonderful," I answered, closing my eyes lazily.

This chick had pulled a serious number on me.

"I'm glad," she responded as she played with a couple of my

locs. After a moment of silence, she said, "You sound sexy when you moan like a girl."

"Girl, stop!" I said with a mixture of shyness and humor. We both laughed a little before I spoke again. "You know, I don't let just anyone do that to me."

"Well, I'm glad to know I'm special enough to have that honor."

I wanted to tell her then that I loved her, but I held it in. Instead, I fell asleep with her in my arms, cocooned in her warmth and her scent.

The next morning, as I looked at the passion mark she had put on my neck, I knew she had not only marked my flesh, but my soul, as well. I had to make her my lady.

Chapter 14
Back on Track

Shanelle

I was on cloud nine.

Falling asleep with J.B. had been what I needed to put my mind and heart at ease. I knew I had been missing her, but I didn't realize how much until we kissed. I could've overdosed on her kisses. I was so in love with this woman.

This woman...

She had touched me in ways I had never thought I could be touched, both physically and emotionally. She had my body and soul soaring the night before. She possessed me.

Then she allowed me to possess her.

I experienced something with her that I had never done before. I had my first real taste of a woman, and I will admit that the experience still had me in awe. At first, I was nervous and a little scared, but I tried not to let her know. I had never even attempted anything of the sort, but I wanted to please her and show her that bringing her joy brought me joy, too.

I wasn't sure of what to expect. I didn't know if I would be able to handle it. I had once heard giving head to a woman being compared to eating oysters, so I feared I would be grossed out by the feel of wetness or sliminess in my mouth. However, it was nothing like that, thank goodness.

I can't begin to describe how it felt to run my tongue along her womanhood like she'd done to me on several occasions before. I don't think I could accurately tell anyone of the power rush I felt when I made her produce deep, yet feminine sounds of pleasure because of what I did to her.

For those who are curious, I want to clear one thing up: It *does not* taste like chicken. Still, I found myself happily drowning in the flavor that was all her. Better yet, she tasted of *us*. I felt I brought about her arousal, so her flavor was *ours*. I wanted to do it again and again.

*****

As I showered the next morning, I was still reveling in what had occurred the previous night. I was wanton and brazen...and deeply, undoubtedly in love.

I was so in love that I wanted to tell somebody, anybody, and everybody.

Yet, I knew I wasn't ready.

But still...

I wanted someone to feel my joy. It turned out I didn't have to say a word.

"Who is it? You can tell me, girl!"

I smiled as I stared at Deniece over my Diet Dr. Pepper. "What are you talking about?" I asked innocently.

"Oh, don't play that mess with me," she said, throwing a balled up napkin at me. "Come on! I'm dying to know. Who's got you beamin' like this?"

"I have no idea of what you mean," I said before taking a sip of my drink. I wanted to tell her so bad, but I knew how she was.

"I won't tell," she offered, as if reading my mind. "Your secret will be safe with me."

"Puhlease!" I said with a laugh. "No secret is safe with you, Niecey! I love you, but you are the mouth of the south."

"I'm offended," she scoffed. "I'm not that bad," she then debated. "You'd be amazed at the stuff I keep to myself."

"I sure would," I said back, "because your ass can't even hold water."

I laughed at her disappointed face.

Her expression changed to one of determination. "I'm gonna find out eventually. I find out everything."

"Well, good luck," I told her with a laugh. I was about to say something else to pick on my friend, but my cell phone rang. I smiled when I looked at my caller ID.

"Hello," I answered with a smile in my voice.

"Hey, baby. How you doin'?"

J.B.'s accent washed over me, and I felt my face get warm.

"I'm good," I answered, sounding more like a teenager with a crush than a grown woman. "How are you?"

"Ooh! That's him, isn't it?" Deniece exclaimed with excitement.

Hearing my friend's exclamation over the phone, J.B. laughed and said, "No. It's *her*."

"True," I said, unable to erase the smile that had found residence on my face. After noticing how closely Deniece was watching me, I straightened up. "What's up?"

"I was just checkin' on you, baby," J.B. responded. "Was thinking about you."

"Oh really?" I asked, failing miserably at trying to sound nonchalant.

"Yes, baby," she replied, her voice dropping an octave. "Have you been thinking about me?"

I couldn't even begin to deny it. "Yes," I answered meekly.

"Yes," Deniece mimicked before taking a sip of her drink.

I stuck my tongue out at her before standing up to continue my call in the ladies' room where there would be more privacy.

"I'll be right back," I informed her.

She waved me off and then picked up her own phone to make a call.

"I didn't mean to take you away from your friend," J.B. said while I made my way to the bathroom.

"It's okay," I told her as I entered the empty bathroom. "She was being nosey anyway. Besides, it's quieter in the ladies' room, and I can give you all of my attention."

"I like that," she said. I could hear the smile in her voice.

"I bet you do," I retorted, laughing. *Lawd, this woman has me as giddy as a teenager.*

"Can I have a little more of your attention this weekend?" she asked me suddenly.

"You can have a lot more tonight," I replied before catching myself.

"Oh, I plan to," she informed me.

I swear, it felt like my kitten purred at her statement.

"But, I have something to ask you," she continued.

"Okay?" I said, unsure of what to expect.

"My family is having a little get-together this Saturday, and I would love for you to come with me."

Meet her family? Was I ready for that? I wasn't sure, but after the brief separation between us, I refused to disappoint her.

"I would love to."

"Really?"

"Really."

We talked for a few more minutes before she told me that she would see me later that evening. Once again, I caught myself wanting to tell her that I loved her. Once again, I refrained.

After ending my call, I made my way back to the table where Deniece feigned sleeping.

"Very funny," I told her as I sat down.

"Well," she began, "it took you long enough."

"I'm sorry," I said, although I really wasn't.

"I just talked to Rayne," she informed me.

Rayne was another soror, who was always "in the know" when it came to events on campus or in town. I already had an idea of what Deniece was about to tell me.

"The Sigmas are having a party Saturday night. Are you game?"

"My bad, chica," I said with just a hint of regret. "I just made plans for Saturday."

"And it's more important than putting in an appearance at this party?" she questioned. "Now I really wanna know who this cat is!"

"None of your business. You are so nosey!"

"And?"

I laughed and changed the subject.

After having lunch with Deniece, I went to the library for a while before heading to my parents' house.

I knew I would be spending the rest of the night with J.B., and I was excited about it. However, I was nervous as hell about meeting her family a few days later.

*****

I spent the next three nights making love to J.B. It was heaven on earth for me. We'd wake up each morning before sunrise and fix breakfast together before taking showers and starting our day. Then, we'd text all day long and talk on the phone as she made her way to my place.

Saturday came way before I was ready for it. I stood in my bedroom staring at my reflection in the mirror. I wanted to look nice, but not over the top. I had changed my clothes several times before finally settling for a yellow baby doll shirt with a white belt, a pair of white leggings, and baby doll slippers. I had taken the time to curl my hair in soft ringlets and applied the lightest coat of make-up. After approving of my appearance, I was ready to meet J.B.'s family...

I'm such a liar; I was terrified!

I tried to appear confident as I looked at my reflection, but my stomach was in knots. I had tried several times to go to the bathroom to relieve my stress in one way or another, but my body refused to cooperate with me.

I was still telling myself to be a big girl when J.B. arrived. She was smiling when I opened the door, but her smile turned into a look of desire as she checked me out from head to toe.

"Hey there, beautiful," she greeted with a smile.

"Hello to you," I replied, returning the smile. She almost made me feel bashful with the look in her eyes.

"Are you almost ready?" she asked.

"Yes," I answered. "I just need to grab my purse."

Before I could walk away, she pulled me to her and kissed me deeply.

"Go ahead and grab your stuff," she said, backing away from me. "I'll wait in the car."

I nodded and made my way into my room to get my belongings. After that kiss, I didn't even want to go anywhere. I would have preferred to just stay inside with her. However, I had told her that I would go with her and meet her family.

As I locked my front door, I took a deep breath and prayed nothing would go wrong on this trip.

As we rode on the interstate, the music from J.B.'s system played quietly in the background. I looked out of the window, watching cars fall behind us as J.B. maneuvered through the traffic.

"Are you nervous?" she asked, pulling me out of my private thoughts.

"No," I replied quickly before sighing. "Okay, maybe a little," I admitted.

"Don't be," she said with a chuckle.

She took my hand and brought it to her lips. The contact immediately sent fire running through my veins.

"My family is just like any other family, baby. Relax."

"Easy for you to say," I told her. The more I thought about what was about to happen, the more nervous I got. I had given tons of speeches, participated in pageants, and emceed many functions, but never had I been as nervous as I was when we pulled into the driveway of Drs. Gerald and Josephine Donovan. I then noticed several cars parked along the street in front of the residence. My stomach immediately felt like it had balled up into a tight knot, but I tried not to let J.B. know of my apprehension.

As we walked towards the front door, I took in the large manicured yard with the small fountain at its center. Though the house wasn't quite big enough to be called a mansion, it was not a small home by any means.

J.B. opened the front door, ushering me in before her.

"Knock, knock," she said loudly as music from another room floated in the air. She then took me by my hand and led me into the living room where several of her relatives were already entertaining each other.

We were greeted with several 'heys' and 'hellos', and I shook several hands after J.B. introduced me as her friend Nelle. I smiled at the nickname she had given me, and then blushed as I privately remembered how she called me *her Nelle* when we made love.

The thought of our nights of intimacy eased the tension in my body as I replayed a moment in my mind that was beyond inappropriate at the moment. That brief moment of ease immediately vanished when we entered the kitchen and J.B. uttered the one word that struck fear into my heart.

"Mama!" she said with pleasure, leaving my side for a moment to hurry to her mother and kiss her on the cheek.

She then ushered me over to the pretty brown-skinned woman

who bore an amazing resemblance to songstress Anita Baker. Her smile was kind and genuine as J.B. introduced us.

"Mama, this is my friend Shanelle Carter." She introduced me almost as if she were filled with pride to show me off. She then looked at me and said, "This beautiful woman is my mother, Mrs. Josephine Donovan."

"It's a pleasure to meet you, Mrs. Donovan," I said, smiling. I held my hand out to shake her hand, but she surprised me by pulling me into a welcoming embrace.

"Everybody around here calls me Jo," she said, smiling back. "None of that Mrs. Donovan stuff. I'm not that old yet."

"Yes, ma'am," I responded with a chuckle.

"Where's Daddy?" J.B. asked her.

It tickled me to hear her refer to her dad as 'daddy'. It added a cute softness to her.

"He should be home soon," she answered. "He had to do an emergency c-section."

"Oh, okay," J.B. said with a nod. "Well, I have a few more people to introduce Nelle to, and then I will be back to eat all of your food up."

"Oh, I know it," her mother replied with a laugh. She then looked at me and said, "We will have girl talk before you go."

"Yes, ma'am," I told her with a serious nod.

"Don't worry," she said. "We don't bite around here. Make yourself at home."

I was instantly put at ease with her.

The rest of the evening seemed to fly by. I met several of J.B.'s aunts, uncles, and cousins. I even met the one who was at the movie theater with her, much to J.B.'s amusement. It might have been funny to J.B., but it damn sure wasn't at the time.

Slowly, one by one, everyone began to leave. J.B. and I stuck around and helped straighten the kitchen back up. It had been a night of good food, good music, dominos, and spades. I had enjoyed my time with J.B.'s family and maybe even envied their closeness a little bit.

Though I was definitely well loved in my family, we didn't have the kind of bond that was so evident with J.B.'s family. We didn't have many get-togethers because my mother didn't want anything to turn up missing or risk getting something spilled on the carpet. Okay, so my family was a little bourgeoisie. I admit that. I can also admit that I could get used to enjoying evenings with the Donovans.

Gerald Donovan, better known as Gerry by the family, was an intelligent man who had a quick and crazy sense of humor that quickly let people know he hadn't forgotten his humble beginnings as an inner city child in the Bronx. He and Jo shared the story of how they met and how after many years she had convinced him to move down south.

I found myself as enchanted by J.B.'s parents as I was by her.

Once we were in the car, J.B. remembered she had left something inside. I sat in the car and reflected over the evening. Everything about J.B. made me feel more strongly for her. With every passing moment, I wanted to be hers. But, I was still afraid. In a moment of twisted humor, I thought to myself that at least I had met one family who would accept me.

I smiled to myself as J.B. got back in the car.

"What are you smiling for?' she asked, looking at me.

"I really enjoyed tonight," I told her. "You have a wonderful family."

"Thank you," she said, returning the smile. "They like you, too."

"Do you really think so?" I asked.

"I know so," she replied. "My mom says she thinks you are a sweet girl and that you must be something special because I brought you over."

"Is that a big deal?" I wanted to know.

"Honestly," she began, "you are only the second woman that I've ever brought home. So, yes, that's a very big deal."

"Well, I feel very special," I replied with sincerity.

"You are," she said in a tone that made my heart beat faster.

The ride back to my place seemed to take forever. No more words were spoken once we left the Donovan's driveway.

No words were necessary as we entered my apartment and immediately started to undress each other. There was no music, no world outside. There were only the sounds of our breathing, our moans of pleasure, and words of affection that paled in comparison to the depth of my true feelings for my lover.

I loved her.

I silently said it with every kiss that I shared with her. Every caress of my fingers whispered 'I love you' against her skin. Every moan that burst from my throat to my lips and into the air screamed that I loved her. Love flowed from my soul as she tasted and drank from my womanhood. Even the scratches on her shoulders from my tight grip were laced with my love for her. As she strapped up and slid deeply inside of my cavern, my body screamed my feelings. Each time she dipped into my femininity and I called her name, I heard myself saying 'I love you'.

But, I never said it aloud.

She responded to every touch, every gesture, every moan, and every hard breath. Her body communicated with mine, and we conversed through our lovemaking, saying with our flesh what we were both too afraid to say with our mouths. Yet, I understood what her body screamed with clarity as we came together...

I love you, too...

We lay in the bed saturated with passion and sweat, but sated for the moment. I had slowly begun to drift to sleep in the comfort of her arms, when I heard her speak.

"I want more."

"Huh?" I nuzzled closer to her. "More what?" I asked, looking up at her with sleepy eyes.

"More of you," she answered, and then surprised me. "I think it's time, Nelle. Will you be my lady?"

Chapter 15
My Lady

J.B.

She lay quietly, but I could feel her heartbeat pounding against my skin.

"Your lady?" she repeated slowly as if tasting the concept for the very first time.

"Yes," I replied. "My lady. My woman. My mate. My girlfriend."

After another moment of quiet, she spoke. "This is so sudden. I don't know what to say."

"It's simple," I said quietly. "Yes or no."

"It's not that simple," she responded back. "This is still so new to me—"

"It can't be new forever," I interrupted. I grabbed a hold of my emotions before speaking again. "Look, I know this is a big change for you, but it can be a good change for the both of us. Don't you enjoy being with me?"

"Of course, I do," she answered, intertwining her fingers with mine as if to solidify her point. "You know I do."

I brought her hand to my lips and kissed each fingertip.

"Do you like when I kiss you?" I asked as I felt her body start to respond to my caressing.

"I love it," she answered sultrily.

Her breathing quickened when I released her hand and slowly ran my fingertips along her stomach before finding moisture between her thighs.

"Don't you like when we make love?" I asked as I began to slowly stroke her wetness.

By then, she couldn't even speak. She could only nod her head and allow a soft moan to escape her lips. I caught the sound between my own lips as I pulled her in for a kiss that left us both breathless for a moment.

"I want you," I whispered against her lips while rolling her onto her back.

"I want you, too," she said with a whimper as I placed a passion mark on the silky skin of her neck.

"I want you to be mine."

I spoke the words against her skin as I slid two fingers deep inside of her. She moaned my name, and the need to even speak evaporated. I found myself drowning in the sound of her moans as they mixed with my own. I let myself get inebriated as I drank the nectar between those satin thighs.

We touched and tasted each other, and came again and again. If my dick had been homegrown, I'm sure she would've gotten pregnant.

As I drifted off to Slumberville, I remembered she hadn't answered me. I decided to let her sleep on it. I didn't want to push her, but I knew what I wanted, and it was her. I would give her time to think it over, but as I stepped into her shower the next morning, I prayed she wouldn't think too much or for too long. Just as I stepped out of the shower, I heard her cell phone ring. As I dried off, I ear hustled.

"Hello," I heard her say. "Yeah, girl, I'm so sorry. I didn't get in until late and I was occupied...none of your business!" She then laughed. "Yes, I was with my mystery boo. You are so nosey...You came by this morning?...I was knocked out. I had a long night...none of your business! Girl, hush!...Well, when you figure out where you've seen it before, then you tell me...Bye, nosey. I'm hanging up on you now."

I heard her chuckle after ending her call. When she tipped into the bathroom, I was nearly dressed. I was brushing my teeth with the toothbrush that had found its way into the holder next to hers.

Dressed in just a pink silk robe, she joined me at the sink to brush her teeth, also. As we stood side by side, I knew I could easily get used to waking up every morning and doing this ritual with her. Hell, I wanted to.

After taking care of our oral hygiene, I buttoned up my shirt and watched as she set the shower for herself. I then reached for her and pulled her close to me.

"Well?" I asked.

"Well?" she repeated.

I didn't want to push, but I couldn't help it. "Are we gonna make this official or what?"

She was quiet for a minute. "This will be a huge transition for me," she began. "I'm still adjusting to this. I've never been in a relationship with a woman, J.B."

"I know that," I told her. "I'm not asking you to start wearing rainbow gear and sing show tunes. I'm just asking you to be my lady. I want to be able to spend the night without having to slip away before sun-up. I want to take you out of this apartment, treat you like more than just a lover."

She was quiet, almost like she was lost in thought.

I continued, "I introduced you to my family to show you that you can be with me and it be alright."

"Not everybody is as welcoming as your family," she debated. "Some people are hateful and cruel."

"But not everybody," I argued gently. I hugged her and held her close to me. "I'll be with you every step of the way. I will do all

I can to protect you from the bullshit."

She was quiet for a moment. Her fear was understandable. I felt the same kind of apprehension before. However, I had been alone. She had me.

"Can you see yourself with me?" I asked her suddenly.

"Yes, I can," she answered without hesitation.

"Then let's make it happen," I whispered, kissing her on those soft lips. "Let me love you."

I heard her quick intake of breath and could feel her heart racing.

"Do you love me?" she asked shyly.

"Yes," I admitted to her. "I love you."

"Really?" she said.

I could've sworn I saw her eyes glisten.

"Yes," I answered. " Let me show you how much. Be my lady, Nelle."

She nodded her head and whispered, "Okay."

"Okay?" I responded, feeling a smile spread across my face. I was ready to celebrate, but I paused. "Are you sure? Do you really want this?"

"Yes," she responded before bringing those lips back to me.

We stood there in her bathroom for several minutes, kissing and hugging. It was almost ridiculously sweet, but I had no complaints. I was ecstatic.

Shanelle Carter was my lady.

We were official.

After a few more moments of cuddling and nuzzling, I stepped out of the bathroom so she could shower in private. After two minutes of hearing the water, I found myself going into the bathroom and stepping into the small cubicle fully dressed. Within moments, I went from kissing her to balancing her thighs on my shoulders while I devoured every ounce of her wetness. I was high from her taste, her sounds, the feel of her fingers tangled in my locs. I was in heaven, and I was taking my lady with me.

My lady.

As I lay her damp body on her bed and licked her from her collarbone to the tips of her toes, I reveled in the fact that I was making love to my lady.

My Lady.

As I kissed her forehead while she slept several orgasms later, I was still smiling about the fact that she had said yes.

A couple months later, I was still basking in the fact that this beautiful, intelligent woman was mine. Over the course of those few months, things were going beautifully.

We spent many nights together, either at her place or mine. Nearly each night was spent making love. She touched and pleased me in ways I had never allowed another woman to. Our mornings were spent catering to each other. She'd cook for me, or I'd flaunt my cooking skills.

I was happy.

Don't get me wrong; things weren't perfect. She still had her issues, so we kept PDA to a minimum. However, people were beginning to take notice of the fact that we were together often.

She had even started catching a little slack from her sorors. Though it was still unsettling for her, she dealt with it as well as she could. I didn't even sweat it when she told them that we were "close friends".

Okay, so I take that back. It *did* bother me a little bit, but it was a different scenario when we went somewhere out of the way or if we were with my family and close friends. She was the perfect girlfriend, and those were the moments that made my issues with her seem small to me.

She even started spending time with my family, having Thanksgiving and Christmas dinner with us. I would joke with her about how she was just with me because she liked my mother. They had even had lunch few times without me.

I introduced her to Jazz, and ultimately got my friend's approval in private. We even went on a few double dates. Things were going well.

Maybe too well.

Chapter 16
Bad Decisions

Shanelle

In hindsight, I knew I was messing up.

Honestly, I knew I was messing up beforehand. I pondered over my decision again and again. My stomach was in knots as I stared at my cell phone. That should've been my first indication that this was a horrible idea.

J.B. would be furious with me, but I didn't know what else to do. I thought I had been doing a good job of opening up and moving forward with my relationship with her. Things were going great.

She treated me like a princess. I couldn't remember ever feeling so loved, and I wasn't afraid to give her my love in return. Saying I love you was as easy as breathing, and it took my breath away each time we told each other.

Now my love was being tested.

As I stared at my phone, I tried to talk myself out of making the call.

"Stop being a coward and do the right thing," I scolded myself. "Do the right thing."

But, even as I said these things, I found myself pressing the 'talk' button and placing the call that I would soon regret.

Chapter 17
Heartbreak

J.B.

"Has anybody heard from Derrick?" I asked a few staff members of the newspaper. "He's supposed to cover that ceremony sponsored by the A.K.A's tonight."

For a minute, no one said anything. They just looked at me like I had messed up.

"What?" I wanted to know.

"Did you forget?" said Stephani, my co-editor.

"Forget what?"

"Derrick had to go out of town," she told me. "You're supposed to cover it tonight for him, remember?"

"Damn!" I exclaimed.

I had forgotten. I had been so focused on my relationship that I'd been slacking a little bit in all other aspects of my life. I hadn't even been kicking it with my friends as much. I needed to get back on track.

"Okay, okay. I'm on it. Did he leave any info on it at all?"

"It should be in your box," Stephani answered, shaking her head at me.

I checked my box, and there were several items that had accumulated over a couple of days. This was bad business on my part. When working in the media, everything is time-sensitive. I silently vowed to get it together.

I thumbed through the papers and separated my essentials from the unnecessary. I came across the itinerary for the ceremony and glanced over the information Derrick had left behind. One of the recipients caught my eye.

For outstanding service in the community: Shanelle Carter.

I didn't even know she was receiving one of the awards.

I immediately picked up my phone to call her. After ringing for half a minute, it went to voicemail. I knew she had a hair appointment, so I just left a message for her.

"Hey baby. I was just going over some stuff for tonight, and I came across something that said you're receiving an award tonight. How come you didn't tell me? Anyway, I'm covering it, so I guess I will see you tonight. I love you."

I ended the call and took care of a little office work. Afterwards, I went home and quickly found something appropriate to wear for the event. A feeling of apprehension came over me after I called Nelle again and got no answer.

Since I had to meet with the photographer before the ceremony began, I had to be there early. On my way to the hall, I stopped by Nelle's. Her car was parked out front, but there was no answer at the door. I used the key she had given me to unlock the door. Upon entering, I found she was gone. I locked the door and headed to the hall, calling her one more time on the way. This time, the call went straight to voicemail, causing me to become officially irritated.

I tossed my Bluetooth into the passenger seat and turned the music up loud while driving the rest of the way to my destination. James, the photographer, was waiting for me when I entered the building. We discussed a few of the shots that I wanted him to get for the article, and then we went our separate ways to mingle for a bit. More people entered the auditorium, and for a while, I didn't see her, but when I did, she took my breath away.

She was dressed in an apple green dress that hugged her body as closely as I did at night. She accessorized with pink jewelry and a pearl necklace to pay homage to her sorority. Her hair fell in soft waves around her shoulders. Her make-up was flawless, and for a moment, I could only gaze at the beautiful lips I had kissed that morning. She looked like she had just stepped out of a fashion magazine.

I was about to wave to get her attention, but someone else beat me to it.

I watched with disbelieve and instant hurt as Travis moved to her side and escorted her towards someone who wanted both of their attention. Going by the resemblance, I knew instinctively that the woman was Shanelle's mother. I was given a glimpse into the future and saw what Nelle would look like in twenty-five years. Her mom was beautiful. There was no denying that great genes ran in her family.

What held my attention was not the beauty of both women, but the closeness between the two of them and Travis. I watched with a tinge of envy as Mrs. Carter placed a kiss on his cheek before watching the seemingly nice couple as they walked away. Anger filled me as I watched the woman who was supposed to be my lady walk down the aisle with the one guy she knew I had a problem with.

My anger turned to agony as the day replayed in my mind. Missed phone calls were really ignored calls. She hadn't even told me that she was getting an award. How long had she known? Why the secrecy?

She didn't want me to know because she knew I would want to be her escort.

I had to take a minute in the ladies' room to compose myself.

After the ceremony, I caught up to her in the foyer of the

auditorium. The surprise on her face was almost comical. Had my emotions not been so fucked up, I probably would've laughed.

"So, Ms. Carter," I began professionally, "how did it feel to be the recipient of an award tonight?"

For a second, she didn't respond.

"Cat got your tongue?" I asked coolly.

"J.B.—" she began, but I cut her off.

"Don't, Shanelle," I said, not able to look at her for a moment. "Let's just get this over with."

"J.B.—"

"How does it feel to be a recipient of one of tonight's awards?"

She sighed and gave the appropriate response about how honored she was and blah, blah, blah. After thanking her, I made my preparation to walk away.

"J.B., please let me explain," she said, grabbing my arm as I turned away.

"I don't want you to," I replied. "Let me go so we don't cause a scene. I know you wouldn't want that."

She slowly loosened her grip.

"Can we please talk later?" she asked.

For a split second, I lost my cool. "You had all fuckin' day to talk to me," I snapped. I caught a hold of my temper before saying, "Don't you have a date waiting? Why don't you go and talk to him?"

I walked away, refusing to turn around because I didn't want to see the look on her face. Even more so, I didn't want her to read the hurt on mine. Instead of going home, I went straight to the office, wrote the article, and then went to an off-campus bar to have a couple of beers. It was after two a.m. when I made it home. When I saw a light on, I knew she was there. It took everything in me to go inside. She was sitting on my sofa as if she belonged there. At one point, I thought she did.

"Where have you been?" she asked, standing up to walk over

to me.

"It's none of your concern," I replied, walking past her to get a drink out of my fridge.

"Are we going to talk about this like adults?"

"Like adults?" I challenged with a laugh. "Were you being an adult when you went the entire fuckin' day iggin' my calls?"

"Baby, let me explain—"

"There is nothing for you to explain," I interrupted, slamming my drink on my countertop. "I know why you did it already. You didn't want to be seen with me on your side. You made me feel like a muthafuckin' lame tonight. Why the fuck are you here with me anyway? Shouldn't you be celebrating somewhere with your boy, Travis?"

"I'm here because I love you," she answered quickly.

"No," I argued. "*I* love *you*. There is almost nothing that I wouldn't do for you. But, you weren't even woman enough to tell me that you were embarrassed to be seen with me."

"I'm not embarrassed!" she yelled. "I'm still scared!"

"Then you aren't ready for a real relationship with me," I said quietly.

The sudden silence was deafening.

"What are you saying, J.B.?" she asked. A look of dread covered her face.

"Go home, Shanelle."

"What do you mean, J.B.?"

She was in my face, but I couldn't look her in the eyes.

"Please, Shanelle."

"Please what?" she demanded.

She was in my face, grabbing me, trying to get me to look at her. I had never seen her this confrontational.

"Let's work this out," she pleaded.

"You want to work this out?" I challenged her.

I looked at her and saw her eyes glistening. Then I walked over to where her cell phone sat on my coffee table, picked it up, and handed it to her.

"Pick anybody in your contacts," I told her. "Call them up and tell them that you're with me. Call your mom or one of your sorors and tell them that you love J.B. Donovan. Jocelyn Brianna Donovan."

She stared at her phone for a minute. I watched as a tear fell from her eye.

"Go home, Shanelle. I love you, but you're not ready for me. I refuse to hide in the closet with you. I can't do this."

I walked into my bedroom and closed the door behind me. I leaned against it, and my heart ached as I listened to her shed tears in my living room. A few minutes later, I heard my front door open and close.

And that was it.

My lady had just walked out my door and out of my life. I lay in my bed and did something I couldn't recall ever doing.

I curled up and cried myself to sleep.

Chapter 18
Foolish

Shanelle

Hospital food.

That is what I had equated my life to. It had become bland. It lacked in spice and flavor. And just like hospital food, I was only sustaining.

Existing.

Gone was the vibrant go-getter that had been only weeks before. Gone was the go-getter that I had been my entire life. All it had taken was losing J.B. I had never been in such a slump over a breakup. Then again, I had never really been in love before.

I now knew what it was like to be heartsick. I lost my baby. I lost my heart. No. I had given up my baby. I could've prevented all of my self-inflicted agony if I had just been honest with her. Better yet, if I would've been honest with myself and said to hell with what others may think. But, I was afraid, and it cost me what was most important to me. The deed was done. My love for her had been tested.

And I had failed miserably.

After a week of unanswered calls and texts, I finally gave up on trying to communicate with her. She was done with me.

She once told me that she would protect me from the bullshit, but she had left herself wide open and hadn't been protected from *me*.

I was plagued with guilt because I knew I had failed her, failed us. I knew I hurt her. I saw it in her eyes at the banquet before she went cold on me. I had seen it in her eyes when she told me to go home that night.

I should've stayed. I should've fought for her and our relationship. I should've followed her into her room and did whatever it would've taken to get her to listen to me.

But, I hadn't.

My life seemed so empty without her. There was no color. The things that had amused me before I met her no longer sparked an interest. I didn't want to go out. I didn't want to be social. I stayed away from my sorors because I didn't want to deal with the "what's wrongs" that I knew they would drill me with.

I spent the weeks following my breakup comforting myself with take-out food, wine coolers, and junk food. My body was paying for it, too. In the few long weeks I had been away from J.B., I had gained almost five pounds.

I knew I needed to snap out of it, but it was so hard. I was lost without her.

*****

"You really need to get out of this apartment."

I looked up from where I lay on my sofa. Deniece was standing over me.

"How'd you get in?" I asked her groggily.

"It was open," she answered.

Damn. I was really tripping to leave my door unlocked. I never did that.

"Girl, you really need to get over him."

"Get over who?" I asked, remaining where I lay.

"Your mystery guy," she answered.

If only she knew.

"But you wanna know the truth," she began, crouching down so we were more leveled. "I don't think it's a guy at all."

Busted.

"What?" I sat up quickly enough to make her stumble a little before standing upright. "What are you talking about?"

"I've been seeing you with the newspaper editor," she said. "And she is *clearly* a lezzie-"

"A lezzie?" I interrupted, almost indignant.

"It's cool," she said quickly. "I mean, if you swing that way, that's your business—"

"Well, I don't," I lied quickly and almost cringed at the non-truth. "J.B. and I were just friends."

"*Were?*" Deniece questioned. I ignored her raised eyebrow.

"Yes," I responded as I stood up. I stretched before making my way to the kitchen.

Deniece followed and watched quietly as I made myself a heaping bowl of chocolate ice cream.

"Soooo, what happened to put your friendship status in the past tense?" she asked.

"We had a disagreement," I answered, trying to sound blasé as I concentrated on topping my ice cream with Hershey's syrup.

"A disagreement?" she repeated. "In other words, you two broke up."

"Nieci!" I exclaimed. "Seriously?!"

"Seriously, my ass, Shay," she threw back at me. "You go from being seen with her quite a bit to not at all. You've been like a sick puppy for weeks. You haven't been out with the sorors, and you've barely even been talking to me."

"That's because you talk too damn much," I snapped.

I didn't mean for it to come out the way it did, and I instantly felt bad when I looked at my friend's expression.

"I'm sorry, Nieci."

"Don't be," she said, holding up her hand. Her voice was quiet when she spoke again. "I know you think that I'm always running my mouth, but it only seems that way because I tell *you* everything. However, I would *never* put your business in the streets. But, the crazy shit is, I don't have to say anything. This campus is small as hell when it comes to gossip and speculation. People see and people talk."

I was silent for a minute before saying, "We were just friends."

"You know what?" she started, sounding frustrated with me for the first time. "If that is what you need to tell yourself to sleep at night, then so be it. But, I know it's bullshit, okay?"

I sat down at the table and tried to act aloof as my friend continued to drill me.

"Whether you believe it or not, I can read you like a book," she said. "We've been friends for years, and I consider you as more of a sister than just a soror. Everybody seems to kiss your ass, but I'm not going to do it. I've always been real with you, and now is no different. I'm calling you out on your bullshit. If you're in love with a girl–and it's written all over your face–that's your biz. It's not my place to judge you, and personally, that means there are more men available for me. You can keep trying to play it off, but the only person you're playin' is yourself."

I was so stunned by her affirmation that I couldn't speak.

"And furthermore," she continued, "if you don't get over it or fix it, you're gonna be big as a damn house from drowning yourself in this damn junk food."

In spite of her scolding, she gave me a hug and said, "Call me when you get it together, girl."

She grabbed her purse from the living room and left me sitting in the kitchen feeling stupid, but thoughtful. If she could read me, who else could? More importantly, why did it matter?

It didn't matter. J.B. was already gone.

I saw the first teardrop land in my ice cream, then another. As the stream continued, I told myself that I had to get over this shit. I went and got my phone, and did what I thought any other woman in my position would do.

I called Travis.

A couple of hours later, I was presentable in my make-up, freshly flat-ironed hair, and yellow Apple Bottom mini dress. A pair of yellow sandals with four-inch heels set off my look. I looked more like myself than I had in a while.

As I looked at my reflection, I remembered how much J.B. liked seeing me in yellow. The thought was enough to make me head back to my closet to find a change of clothes, but the knocking that came from my front door aborted my mission. It was too late to change clothes now. I shook my head at myself as I went to open the front door.

Travis greeted me with a hello and an appreciative smile. I smiled back and stepped aside so he could come inside.

"You look great," he told me with a smile that grew bigger by the second.

"Thank you," I told him, thinking I may have overdone it a little bit with the mini-dress. "Let me grab my jacket and purse, and I'll be ready."

After getting my necessities, I met Travis at the front door. I allowed him to lock the door before escorting me to his white Honda Accord. I smiled as he opened my door for me and closed it once I had settled into my seat.

I liked the fact that he was always a gentleman and always regarded me with the utmost respect. We always had interesting conversations, and he had a nice sense of humor. We had similar tastes in many areas. Had it not been for meeting J.B., it might've been possible for something deeper to develop between Travis and me if we had tried to date again. But, she had ruined me for anyone else.

Travis and I ended up going to a nice club to listen to a local R&B group do a couple of live sets. As we sat at the bar sipping on a couple of alcoholic beverages, I thanked him for the night out.

"I really needed this," I informed him over the music.

"I'm glad I could be here for you," he said. "You've seemed a little down and out lately."

"I know," I admitted. "I've been going through a little rough patch, but I'm working on it."

"We all go through them from time to time," he said. "But know that you don't have to go through it all alone. You still have friends like me who care a lot about you. I'm here for you."

I smiled at him. "Thank you. I appreciate you for that."

"Nothing to thank me for," he replied. "That's what friends are for, right?"

"Right," I said back with a small smile before taking a long sip of my Long Island Iced Tea.

We listened to the band perform a few more songs. Then I excused myself to go to the ladies' room. On my way, I bumped into a woman and looked up into a face that looked so much like J.B. that I did a double take. After realizing she wasn't J.B., I apologized and continued to the bathroom.

Why couldn't I let go?

My mood for the rest of the night had been altered from that point. I tried to keep on a happy face as we left the club, and I was doing a decent job of it until Travis decided to become nosey.

"Are you going to tell me what's going on with you?" he asked once we were secure in his car.

"Just…life," I answered.

I silently prayed he would accept my answer and start the damn car. No such luck.

"You've been so different lately," he said. "I don't like seeing you like this."

After a minute of not responding, I broke. Before I could catch myself, I found myself crying on his shoulder.

"Whoa," he said, rubbing my back. "Whatever it is will be okay."

"No, it won't," I said, sniffling against his shoulder. "Take me home please."

He did as I asked, saying nothing during the ride, and I appreciated that. Once we got to my place, he escorted me inside and led me to my sofa where we sat quietly for a moment.

He then asked again, "What's going on with you?"

I'm not sure if it was the three drinks I had consumed or if it was just the need to finally tell someone, but I took a breath and told Travis everything from the first time J.B. and I spoke to each other until the event that unfolded that night after the banquet. I even told him how I felt about her.

When I finally finished speaking, he was quiet for a minute.

"So," he began slowly, "I couldn't get any play, but this chick just came along and took you away from us, huh?"

I looked up at him and saw he was smiling. I attempted to smile back.

"It wasn't like I planned for it to happen," I told him. "I don't hate men or anything like that. I just love *her*."

"Wow," he said with a soft snort. "I remember when I couldn't even get the time of day from you."

"That's because you were trying to get the time of day from all of my sorors," I told him with a laugh.

"But I only wanted it from you," he confessed quietly.

The laugh that attempted to come from my mouth was cut short when I realized he was serious.

"You're not playing," I said aloud.

"I'm being very real with you," he replied, looking down at me.

For a moment, neither of us said anything.

A feeling close to panic briefly crept over me as he slowly

leaned towards me. I knew what he was about to do, and he moved slowly enough to give me time to decline his advancement, but I didn't.

I let him kiss me, and I kissed him back.

I waited for the fire to course through me as it had done with J.B., but it never happened. However, his kiss was gentle and pleasant enough, and in that moment, it was exactly what I thought I needed.

It had been weeks since I had received or given any affection. Though he paled in comparison to J.B., he was there, and I knew he genuinely cared for me. He was willing to give me solace after I had confessed my secret and shared my heartache.

Maybe he was taking advantage of the situation, but I couldn't get upset because the truth was I was using him, too.

I used him to try to fill a void that had been left in me several weeks before when I pushed J.B. out of my life. I opened my body up to him and allowed him to invade my personal space in hopes of eradicating the brand that J.B. had put on my body, heart, and soul.

His grunts of pleasure seemed surreal and out of place. I wanted to hear J.B.'s sighs of pleasure, and his were less than a substitute. Though he was well endowed and seemed to be passionate, he did nothing for me. However I played along for his benefit. My moans were doctored and came across as fictitious in my own ears, but he didn't seem to notice as he slowly pounded into me, sharing his version of making love.

Half an hour passed before he was sated, and I was grateful when he helped me up from where we laid on my living room floor. As he dressed, I quickly did the same. I escorted him to the door and thanked him for the evening, the ear, and the nightcap. I tried to pour an ounce of affection into our goodnight kiss before closing and locking my front door behind him.

As I showered, the constant stream of tears blended with the spray of the water. I had only made things worse for myself. I felt like less of a woman for giving myself to a man who I didn't desire in a half-hearted attempt to get over the woman I loved.

I felt like such a fool and, once again, I had no one to blame but myself.

Chapter 19
Moving On

J.B.

I smiled a little as the ball went through the hoop and the tattered net.

"J.B. Donovan is a monster today! Take that shit!" Jazz was talking mad shit to our competition.

The sunny March day was warmer than expected, so some friends called Jazz and me up to shoot a few games in the park. It had been a while since I'd been social, so I gave in and met up with my crew, ready to play. Truth be told, I needed to relieve a little stress and a few games of ball would help. At least for a little while, it would get my mind off of Shanelle.

It had been a month since we split up, and I still missed and craved her. I buried myself in my classes, the newspaper, and making paper. I had become a robot, a machine, doing everything by rote. I kept to myself most of the time.

Only my mom and Jazz knew the reason why I almost worked myself to death over the past month. I mean that literally. I had gotten to the point where I wasn't even eating. The first couple of weeks without her were pure hell. It took every ounce of willpower that I had to keep from answering her calls and texts. On many occasions, I found myself pulling her number up on my phone, but my wounded pride wouldn't allow me to make the call.

One night I lost the fight with my desire for her. I got in my car and drove to her place, but kept going when I saw *his* car parked next to hers. It was after midnight, and seeing his car there so late had me seeing red.

I wanted to get out of my car, knock on the door, and act a damn fool. But, I had no right to. *I* sent *her* away. It wasn't the other way around. She had wanted to work it out. I hadn't; or so I tried to convince myself.

I was frustrated about it all, so I took my frustration out on my friends, Charmaine and Lyric, on the basketball court. Jazz and I had already beaten them two games to none.

"Y'all not tired yet?" Jazz taunted. "It's gotta be hard as hell to keep takin' these beat downs!"

They talked shit back and forth throughout the third game. I spit a little bit, too, making an effort to enjoy the game and the afternoon. After our third victory, we all agreed to meet at Applebee's for drinks later that evening.

"Wanna hit the club up after Applebee's?" Jazz asked while we made our way to my car.

"Sounds good," I answered. "I need to get out and play for a little bit anyway. It's been a minute."

"That's what's up," she said as we climbed into the car. Once we hit the road, she hit me with the question that I knew she had been itching to ask. "So have you talked to Shanelle yet?"

"Nope," I answered, keeping my eyes on the traffic ahead of us. "I don't plan to either. She made her choice, and I've made mine."

We spent the next ten or fifteen minutes debating on my situation with Shanelle. Jazz was convinced that all I needed to do was talk to her, but I refused to do it.

By the time we pulled up to her apartment, I was relieved to be dropping her off. I didn't need her telling me what to do about my love life, even if she did make sense.

"My relationship with Shanelle Carter is over."

"Whatever you say," Jazz said back nonchalantly. She grabbed her bag from the backseat and closed the passenger door. "See ya tonight."

I hit the interstate and traveled the two exits that separated my best friend's place from my own. Before making it to my house, I stopped at the Hess convenience store that was owned by an Arabic family. After grabbing a Gatorade, I made my way to the counter and made small chitchat with Ahmad, the owner's son who was running the register. I liked him. After being schooled in the U.S. for most of his life, he had become "Americanized" and was much more laid back than his parents.

We had just exchanged a couple of jokes, when the bell chimed from the door being opened. We both paused as we took in the sight before us. Only one word could be used to describe her as she smiled at us.

Thoroughbred.

Thick as cool molasses. Hips for days. Breasts that were full and made for touching and sucking. She knew she was bad as hell. I was sure her hair wasn't homegrown, but it didn't matter. The wavy tresses flowed nearly to her small waist. The skirt of her purple Coogi mini dress could barely contain the fullness of her ass. Her brown skin was flawless…smooth thighs and shapely calves. The Jimmy Choo sandals that showcased her pedicured feet screamed "high maintenance".

She walked like she knew she was the shit. As her eyes caught mine and lingered for a moment, I agreed with the thought. A saxophone should've been playing in the distance as she walked.

As she turned around to continue with her task, Ahmad said, "It's moments like this when I love my job."

"I feel you on that," I responded before bidding him adieu.

I walked out of the store but lingered for a minute, leaning against my car and taking a swig of my drink just to have another opportunity to look at the goddess before going home.

The eye contact was immediate once she came out of the store. She smiled. In response, I smiled a little and threw my head up a little bit in salute.

She walked towards her car, but then paused, turned around, and slowly walked towards me.

"Hi," she spoke and flashed that smile.

"Hello," I said back to her.

There was a slight pause before she spoke again. "Look, my name is Monique, and I don't usually do this, but..."

She then commenced to give me her telephone number.

I liked the fact that she was bold enough to approach me. It was usually the other way around, so it was a pleasant change for me. We exchanged a few words before she asked if I was going to call her. I assured her that I would.

I watched in approval as she sashayed away. I could hear that jazz tune playing in my head as her hips moved from left to right. She flipped her hair over her shoulder before opening the driver side door of her white Lexus. She looked back and waved her fingertips at me before climbing inside.

As she pulled off, I noticed the rainbow-colored bar just above her license plate that paid homage to gay pride. It was a bonus to know that she was *openly* a member of the gay community. A big plus.

I knew then that I would definitely be giving her a call.

Once I got home, I showered as the soothing sounds of Jill Scott filled my apartment from the living room. After dressing, I grabbed a Heineken from my refrigerator and played a video game until dusk.

Shortly after eight, my cell phone rang. After seeing it was Jazz, I answered.

"'Sup, homie?" I said in greeting.

"Nada," she answered. "Are you about ready? Char and Lyric are already at Applebee's."

"Damn!" I said with a laugh. "They're gettin' it in early! I'll be there in a few."

Twenty minutes later, I was scooping Jazz up from the front of her apartment, and we were off to Applebee's to drink and shoot the breeze with our capadres.

A couple of drinks and hours crept by, and we found ourselves kicking it at a *Ladies at Play* function in the Downtown area. It was a nice mix of fun and sophistication. Beautiful fems, versatiles, the label-less, and well-dressed doms were everywhere, mingling and enjoying one another. The mood was festive without being overbearing. The vibe was definitely grown and sexy.

While talking to an associate, I felt someone tap on my shoulder.

"So we meet again."

I smiled in surprise when I turned around and found Monique smiling at me.

"Indeed we do," I replied.

My friends were quite understanding when I walked away with the beautiful woman to find a quieter place to converse.

Small talk quickly turned into learning details about each other. I found out she did some modeling work and some acting. Apparently, she was doing something right to have the nice car and clothes. I could tell she knew what she wanted in life. She was definitely not a college girl who was unsure of herself.

I quickly mentally chastised myself for the thought and the accidental comparison. I quickly shook it off and continued to enjoy the rest of the evening with Monique.

We found ourselves sitting at a nearby Waffle House, talking until the sun came up. We ended our night with a hug in the parking lot after I escorted her to her car. I told her to let me know that she'd made it home safely, and she promised me that she would. I watched her drive away before getting into my own car to head home.

Once I was safely at my place, I jumped in the shower and let the warm water caress me. The day of basketball had finally seeped into my bones. It had been a while since I'd played, but it was fine. It had been a very good day for me.

I grabbed a bottle of water from my fridge and took it into my bedroom with me. As I plugged my charger into my phone, the 'new message' alert chimed.

"I'm home," flashed across my screen with a smiley face.

"I'm glad u made it safely," I sent back, smiling to myself.

Monique and I exchanged a few more texts.

"R u sleepy?" she sent to me.

"Not really," I texted back to her.

A few moments later, my phone rang. I couldn't help but to smile as her name flashed across the display on my phone. We ended up talking for almost two hours before we finally said goodnight in spite of it being daylight outside.

For the first time in a month, the last thought of my day wasn't about Shanelle.

Chapter 20
Revelations

Shanelle

My life slowly returned to normal. I started focusing on the things that had mattered so much before. My classes, community activities, and my sorority occupied most of my time. Other than my family, social events and Travis took up what was left of my waking hours.

We had started to date each other exclusively at his request. In spite of both of us knowing my true feelings for J.B., I agreed. I needed someone to give me time and attention, and he was always willing. Despite having that one night together, we hadn't been intimate, and he didn't press the issue. He was always a gentleman and chivalrous. In fact, it wasn't much different from the way we were before other than the fact that we cuddled regularly and he hugged me more often. Though he still couldn't fill the void left from my fallout with J.B., he made it hurt a lot less.

There were still nights when I lay in my bed, alone and missing her. There were still moments when I could hear her laughing at something that I said or did. I continued to read her editorials every week, and I could almost hear her talking to me when I read some of them. I missed all of our times together, but it had been nearly five months and I had to move on. I was trying so hard to move on.

Sometimes I felt like I was using my friend. I found it funny that though we were dating, I still couldn't see him as more than a friend. My family regarded him as my boyfriend, as well as my sorors. To everyone around us, we were the quintessential college couple. We were both from well-off families, both well educated, both good-looking, and appeared to be happy in our relationship. We were always expected to be together at social gatherings, and we didn't let anyone down with that.

The only one who seemed to see through my façade was Deniece. Though she played along in public, being the perfect friend and supporting soror, she didn't hesitate to call me out in private, consistently questioning my relationship with Travis. She fussed at me for using him for the comfort that he brought me. She called him a "small bandage for a shredded heart".

"It's going to break that man's heart when you leave him," she argued with me one night as we watched reality television in my living room.

"Who said I was going to leave him?" I countered, hitting her with a throw pillow.

"It's only a matter of time, girl," Deniece retorted. "What does this man do for you that would make him 'the one'?"

"He's very good to me," I said truthfully. "He's always there when I need to talk. He listens, doesn't judge me, and gives me his shoulder to cry on. He's funny and a great conversationalist—"

"Oh puh-lease!" she interrupted, laughing. "That could easily be me! Maybe I should be your girlfriend then!"

"Very funny," I said, rolling my eyes. "You are so not my type."

"But I know who is," she teased.

"Don't you start with that," I warned her, but it sounded weak to my own ears.

"Awe, come on, Shanelle. Why is it so hard to fess up? Do you really think I'm going to put your business out there like that? I already know you and her were an item. I remember when I came over here and her car was parked outside. I knew I had recognized it. Come on! Fess up just once. I put it on my life that I won't tell anyone."

I couldn't help but to laugh. I hadn't heard anyone use putting something "on their life" as a bargaining chip since high school.

"You are a mess," I told my friend.

"Well?" she pressed on. "I already know. I just want to see if you're gonna stop being a wuss and tell me."

I sat for a minute, feigning interest in the commercial on TV. Finally, I spoke.

"Will you drop the subject if I give you what you want?"

"Scouts honor," she answered.

I could hear the excitement in her voice.

"Fine," I said with a sigh. "Yes, Nieci, I was in a relationship with J.B. Donovan. Feel better now?"

"I knew it!" she sang victoriously. "Details! How did y'all hook up to begin with?"

"I didn't promise you all of that," I told her with a slick smile.

"No fair!" she exclaimed. "That's all part of it!"

After making her wait for a few moments, I opened my mouth and began to tell about how we first met. I continued my story all the way up until the breakup. Though there was some sadness in my heart, it didn't hurt as much as I thought it would to confide in my friend. When I finished sharing with Nieci, her face was solemn.

"You still love her," she said with understanding.

"I admit that I do," I replied honestly, "but it's been over for months, and I'm with Travis now."

"That's just it, sistah girl," she said. "You're not *with* him at all. He's with you. How long is that going to be enough for either of you?"

I sighed in resignation. "I don't know," I responded, looking at my friend. "For now, I need the little bit of solace that he gives me. He's here with me despite how I feel about J.B., and I am grateful for that."

"But unfulfilled," she threw back at me. "I wish you could've seen how your face lit up when you talked about her. He doesn't give you that."

"But he gives me comfort," I defended.

"For how long?' she challenged. "Don't get me wrong. I feel where you're coming from, soror. But how long before one of you gets tired of just being comfortable?"

Her words stuck in my mind for the remainder of the night. I fell asleep with conflicting thoughts about the man who I had yet to call my boyfriend. He deserved more than I was giving him, and I deserved more than I was accepting with him. But, I wasn't ready to let it go just yet.

I guess we gave each other something, and that was better than nothing. It wasn't until a week later that I learned he had given me something more.

*****

As I sat on my couch with my knees pulled up to my chest like a child awaiting punishment, I wanted a nice stiff drink. However, in light of my new medication, I knew alcohol was out of the question. I rocked back and forth as tears ran down my face.

My nerves were bad. I was shaken. Hell, I had nearly had an accident on the way home, running a red light in my dazed state.

I wanted to yell.

I wanted to scream.

I wanted to take a bat and beat the hell out of Travis!

My phone chimed, signaling a new text message. I looked at the sender and the message. I read the text through the tears in my eyes.

How bad is it?
Life altering. Send.
WTF?!
Exactly. Send.

I threw my phone down, got up, and paced the floor, unable to keep still. I picked up my phone again to call Travis, but my shaking hands wouldn't allow me to press the send button. Instead, I went into the kitchen and poured myself a glass of milk. I almost laughed at the ripples in the glass caused by the trembling of my hands. I put the glass to my lips and guzzled the drink. My nerves and stomach immediately rejected the drink, causing me to make a mad dash to my bathroom.

My crying continued as I laid my head on my forearms that were positioned on the edge of my toilet. I wept and balled up in the fetal position on my bathroom floor. I don't know how long I laid there, but when I opened my eyes, the sun had set and there was very little light in my apartment other than that from my bathroom.

My body was sore from the unexpected regurgitation, the endless crying, and the passing out on my cold, tiled floor. I stood up and brushed my teeth before stripping my body of my clothing. I then turned my shower on and stepped inside.

As the hot water eased some of my tension, I scrubbed my body until I nearly bruised parts of it. Barely dry, I threw on a sleeping shirt and grabbed my cell phone from the living room.

I had missed a couple of calls and texts, but they were not of any importance to me. There was only one person who I needed to talk to. I found his name in my phone contacts and finally hit the 'send' button. When I got his voicemail, I refused to leave a message. Instead, I decided to text him.

We need to talk. Urgent.

After sending the message, I sat on the edge of my bed and let my thoughts consume me. The shock I had been feeling before had slowly begun to subside. I was still mad at Travis because it was his fault, but I was also to blame. If I had not opened myself up to him, I would not be sitting here trying to figure out what to do with myself. One act committed in sadness and desperation had just changed my life.

The ringing of my doorbell pulled me out of my reverie.

I rose from my bed and went to look out of my peephole. When I saw Travis standing there, I immediately opened the door.

"Hey, babe," he said, giving me a kiss on the cheek as he stepped across the threshold. "I got your text and came over straight from a group session. Is everything okay?"

For a minute, I couldn't open my mouth to speak. A wave of nausea swept over me, and I took a seat on my sofa.

Immediately attentive, Travis rushed to my side. "What's wrong, Shay?" he asked, concern evident in his voice.

When I still didn't speak, he jumped up and came back with a cool, wet towel. As he blotted my face with the towel, I spoke.

"I'm pregnant."

His movements stop. "I'm sorry," he began, "but I could've sworn you said that you're pregnant."

"I did," I responded, taking the towel out of his hand. "You're going to be a daddy."

"Are you sure?" he asked moments later.

I reached for the paper from the doctor's office that stated my pregnancy test had been positive. I handed it to Travis and let him read it for himself.

For a long moment, he said nothing. My nerves were in shambles as I waited for his response to the news. Slowly, his lips parted, revealing his white teeth in a smile that took a ton of weight off of my shoulders.

"I'm gonna be a daddy," he said calmly. Though his demeanor was cool, the smile on his face gave away his excitement.

My nervousness about his reaction quickly dissipated, and I

smiled back at him. "So you're happy about it?"

"I'm beyond happy," he answered, beaming. He rose from where he sat next to me and then pulled me to my feet, also. "What about you?"

"I'm terrified," I answered honestly. "I don't know anything about having a baby."

"Neither do I," he answered, "but we can figure it all out together."

His optimism sparked my own.

"Do you really think so?" I asked him.

"Without a doubt," he answered, pulling me closer. "I think we're going to make an excellent team, beautiful."

I couldn't help but smile back at him. His enthusiasm was infectious.

"You know what?" I told him. "You're absolutely right. We can do this."

He embraced me and placed a gentle kiss on my lips.

That night, I asked him to stay with me. As we lay in the bed, we discussed plans about the baby while he rubbed my belly possessively.

I fell asleep with the thought that I was going to be a mommy floating around in my mind. The more I thought about it, the more excited I became.

The next morning, I kissed Travis and told him to have a good day. After ushering him out of the front door, I immediately ran and grabbed one of my throw pillows and stuffed it under my shirt.

As I looked at my reflection in the mirror, I marveled at the fact that I had conceived a child and was already several months along. I was proof that it only took one time to get pregnant.

My thoughts then went to Travis. I felt like he was going to be a great father. And he was so good to me. I vowed to be better to him and to stop seeing him as a buffer to help me get over J.B.

J.B...

Olivia Renee Wallace

For a brief moment, I fantasized about how she would've reacted to me being pregnant. I quickly shook the thought off. That chapter had ended, and it was time for me to finally let it go. I had a family to build.

I lay back down on my bed just as my phone dinged. I checked the message.

Hey chick. U ok? U got me worried.

I'm fine. Gonna B a mommy. Send.

WHAT?! REALLY?

Yep! Send.

R U happy abt it?

Very. Send.

Well if U happy, I'm happy 4 U.

Thank U ☺. Send.

J.B.'s not gonna like that.

It duznt matter. J.B. is part of my past. Send.

Now it was time to drill that fact into my own head…and heart. It was time for a new beginning.

Chapter 21
News

J.B.

That first night with Monique was the beginning of many late night calls, afternoon lunches, and evening dates. I enjoyed her company and found it refreshing that we could walk around in public while doing something as simple as holding hands.

She was beautiful and classy, but she had edginess about her, too. She was a girl who came from the hood but refused to be a product of it, and I loved that about her. Every now and then, she would come off as a little bit on the bourgeoisie side, but I had no problem humbling her, and she had no issue with me doing it. So, in my opinion, it worked out.

We spent a lot of time cuddling and getting each other hot and bothered, but we didn't become intimate until we had been seeing each other for around two months. However, when we *finally* did, I learned how sexually liberated she could be. She was a beast in the bedroom! Her stamina was unbelievable! She left me worn out each time we had sex. I had done things with her that I had never done with anyone. Very little was taboo when we were behind closed doors.

We had just as much fun outside of the bedroom. When she wasn't away on a photo shoot or doing a bit role, and I wasn't consumed with school and my side gigs, we were partying like pros on the weekends. There were very few places we weren't seen together, and we were quickly becoming the "it" couple in our GLBTQ community.

She had even posed for a flyer that I had created for a party. It had been my pleasure to showcase her awesome body and face on one of my projects.

Truth be told, she had no problem flaunting her goods. Very seldom was she seen in anything that didn't draw attention to her body. Her shorts and skirts always showed off her beautiful legs. Her shirts always displayed a bit of cleavage. As a model, she always looked the part. Her makeup was always perfect. I often teased her about having her entire face tattooed so it could never get messed up.

She was attentive, and I never had to ask her for anything. She seemed to know what I wanted before I even said anything. In the couple of months we had been dating, she quickly adapted to my ways and seemed eager to please me. She made it known that she wanted to take our dating to the next level, but something continued to hold me back.

Though I had finally moved on from my relationship with Shanelle, I wasn't ready to go headlong into another relationship, or so I told myself. However, I did make the best of my time with Monique. I felt like when I was ready for another relationship, she could definitely be the one. I just wasn't ready yet.

"It's because you still want Ms. Carter."

After sharing my thoughts with Jazz, she shared her thoughts with me, as well.

"That's not it at all," I argued as I sat with her in the barbershop, waiting for her turn to get her hair cut.

She had come by and decided to get her hair trimmed after I got edged up.

"I just don't see the need to alter what we already have going or add stress by putting a title on it."

"Because you miss your lady," Jazz added smoothly.

"No, I don't" I said quickly. Maybe too quickly.

"Yeah right," she said back. "Don't get me wrong, pahtna. Monique is bad as hell. If she weren't your chick, I'd happily tap that. But, there is something about her that doesn't do it for you, and I say it is the simple fact that she is not Shanelle."

"Are you serious right now?" I asked her incredulously.

"Dead ass," she answered.

"Come on now," I debated. "Monique is beautiful, has a great personality, and is funny. Her body is killer, and she's a maniac in the bed. Even more important, she's out of the damn closet. What more could I ask for?"

"Shanelle Carter."

"She's still a confused schoolgirl," I argued. "She doesn't even know who she is or what she wants."

"She wanted you," my friend shot back. "And you *still* want her. I don't care what you say. She had you gone, and she still has you."

"You are mistaken, pahtna," I disputed with her. "I am happy where I am, and I am over her."

"Yeah right," she scoffed. "Keep telling yourself that bullshit until *you* believe it, because I damn sure won't."

I couldn't help but to laugh. A minute later, I spoke again.

"Why are you so set on me being with Shanelle anyway? What do you get out of it?"

"I don't get shit out of it," Jazz answered. "But, you were happy with her. I mean genuinely happy. Yeah, she was in the closet, but she was trying. It didn't bother me when she was with you around me and the crew."

"So you have a problem with Monique?" I asked.

"I won't say all that," she answered, "but sometimes she seems a little saditty. I had expected Shanelle to be like that, but she was mad cool. If I have to choose, I'm Team Shanelle all day long, even though she's with that dude now."

"And that's another thing," I then said. "She's with ol' boy."

"That's just because y'all aren't together," my homie said confidently.

"Now how do you know all that?" I challenged, half joking.

She hesitated for a brief moment before answering. "I just know."

Her hesitation immediately caught my attention. "What was that?"

"What was what?" she asked innocently.

"That hesitation," I answered.

"Hesitation?" She emitted a quick laugh. "Don't start trippin'."

"Oh hell naw," I said, shaking my head. "I know you, Jazz. What was that? You're holdin' out on me! What is it?"

"Nothin', dude," she said, unable to look me in the eye now. "You're reachin'," she accused.

"Reachin', my ass," I threw back. "You're hiding something." After a pause and no response from Jazz, I asked, "You talk to Nelle?"

"Does it matter since you're so over her?" she retaliated.

Never before had I ever wanted to put hands on my friend, but suddenly, I was seeing red. I needed to get the hell out of there before things went wrong. So, I stood up and left. If I had opened my mouth to say anything, there was no telling what would've happened.

As I drove on the interstate, I couldn't get over the betrayal. Why the fuck was my best friend keeping in contact with my ex, knowing what I went through with her? Even worse, what was her motive? Jazz could be a slick bitch when she wanted to be, but I never thought she would go behind my back and plot on my woman...I mean, my ex.

Even more pressing in my mind: how in the hell could Shanelle deny me what I wanted from her, but turn around and keep in contact with my friend after she ripped my damn heart out?

Then again, like Jazz had said, why did it even matter if I was over her? And I was over her, right?

To hell with that; betrayal was betrayal. I was pissed off and hurt that my ace of so many years had went behind my back and kept in contact with my ex. I mean, it went against *the code*. We never went behind the other, and as far as I knew, we didn't keep shit from each other. At least I didn't think we ever had until then. Maybe that was naïve on my part.

I drove around for nearly an hour before going home. When I got there, Jazz was on the front step waiting for me.

"You ready to stop acting like a bitch yet?" she asked nonchalantly as I approached the steps.

"Fuck you," I said, walking past her to go to my door.

"Oh, it's like that?" she said with a laugh, getting up to follow me into my house.

I let her follow me inside. At least I could claim self-defense in my home if I killed her.

"Okay, so what was up with the bitch-fit at the barbershop?" she asked, making herself comfortable on my sofa.

"Why the fuck are you keeping in contact with my ex?" I shot back. "That's some shady shit, yo."

"Oh, you're mad for real," Jazz taunted, amused. "When you get pissy, you start with that 'yo' shit. What are you so mad about? Are you really that mad that I still talk to her from time to time? Hell, you're the one who made us friends!"

"It's shady when you hide it and shit," I told her. "Why are you keeping in touch with her? She's my fuckin' ex!"

"You were the fool to break up with her," she responded. "Not me. I tried to reason with you and tell you to work it out with her. You were the fool. I don't see why I had to stop being her friend because you fucked up."

"I fucked up?" I said in surprise. "She played me!"

"She made a mistake," my friend said quietly. "And you did, too, by letting her go."

"So you're a shrink now, huh?" I said, salty. "So what are you planning to do? Pick up the pieces and start where I left off?"

"Hell no!" she replied quickly. "She's cool, but I don't do women with children. I'm not ready for all of that."

"Children?" I said, confused. "She doesn't have any kids."

"Duh!" Jazz said, rolling her eyes. "The one she's pregnant with."

I felt like someone had pulled the rug from under me.

"Pregnant?"

"Yeah," Jazz responded in an exasperated tone. After seeing the look on my face, she paused before asking, "You didn't know?"

I could only shake my head in shock. I felt like a knife had been shoved into my chest, but I played it off as well as I could.

"Damn," I said with a humorless chuckle. "She's pregnant? Damn."

After a minute, I said the only thing that came to mind.

"Damn."

"Are you okay?" Jazz asked, her concern genuine. "All of the color just slipped from your face."

"I'm good," I lied. "I'm just surprised. That's all."

"I thought you knew, chick. You're about the only one who didn't. It's all over campus. It's not like she's hiding it or anything. She's showing pretty good now."

The details that my friend shared made me nauseous. I excused myself and took a few minutes in the bathroom to regain my composure. As I ran a cool, wet towel over my face, this new revelation played over and over in my head.

Shanelle, my Nelle, is pregnant with that dude's baby. Not our child. Hers and his.

I reprimanded myself for my thoughts. She wasn't my Nelle

anymore. She was Travis What's-his-face's woman now. I had never even thought that far into the future when I was with her. All I knew then was that I wanted her and I was happy with her. The idea of kids never crossed my mind, but learning that she was expecting someone's child was doing things to me. It pissed me off. It hurt me. It enraged me. It saddened me.

The thought of her body being touched by anyone other than me infuriated me. But what could I do? We weren't together anymore, and I had no right to be upset. That fact didn't alleviate the pain that had hit me with a brutal force.

I put my game face back on and went into my living room where Jazz sat on my sofa. Quiet. Waiting. Watching.

"What?" I said, uncomfortable with the knowing look she was giving me.

"Are you going to be alright?" she asked.

"I'm good," I answered with bravado. "Why wouldn't I be okay?"

The look on her face said she could easily see through my ruse.

I sighed before speaking. "Okay," I began, "I am shocked by this new development. I'm even a little shook up by it, but I will be okay."

"So you admit you still have feelings for her?"

After a moment, I answered honestly. "Yeah, I do, but she is with ol' boy and pregnant with his seed. So, what can I say or do? I've moved on, and it's even more apparent that she has, too."

"Just like that, huh?"

"Just like that."

We made idle chitchat for a few more minutes before Jazz said that she had to go. I appreciated her tactful self-dismissal. She knew I needed a little time to regain my composure.

I lay on my couch for nearly an hour before my phone rang. With the roller coaster that my emotions had just boarded, I wasn't sure if I was happy or upset when Monique's name popped up on phone's screen.

"Hello?"

"Hey, baby," she said cheerfully. "I have a great idea. How about we have dinner tonight at The Cheesecake Factory and then-"

"I'm sorry, boo," I interrupted. "I'm not really feeling up to going out tonight."

"Oh, poor baby," she cooed. "Do you want me to come over and heal you up a bit?"

"Not tonight," I answered while running my hand over my face. "I'm going to make it an early night and try to wake up on the right side of the bed in the morning."

"Oh, okay."

I could hear the disappointment in her voice with those two words, as well as the sad goodbye she gave me before I disconnected the call.

Not even strawberry cheesecake and wild sex could make this night better for me. After my shower and a Heineken, I laid in my bed.

For the first night in months, my *only* thoughts before falling asleep were of Shanelle.

Chapter 22
Hello, Again

Shanelle

I stood in the mirror and checked out my appearance.

My face was fuller, but then again, so was the rest of my body. While the roundness of my belly had taken some getting used to, the extra fullness of my breasts was a welcomed addition.

I smiled as I looked at my reflection. Aside from the obvious changes, I was glowing. I was content. In a couple of months I was going to be a mommy. Who would've ever seen any of this in my future? I certainly hadn't, at least not so soon. However, I had no complaints. I figured everything happened for a reason. So, I went with the flow.

My family's reaction was a pleasant surprise. My father was happy, and my mother was ecstatic at the thought of becoming a grandmother. Only weeks after I told them that Travis and I were expecting, they began renovating one of their guestrooms to turn it into a nursery.

Everything was going well. I made it through my first two trimesters without much trouble. I did things I had never done before, like putting myself on WIC and getting my very first EBT card. Though my parents told me that they would take care of everything, I wanted to do more than raise my child off of my trust fund. I started a job as a customer rep online to make my own income. I was determined for Travis and I to handle it, but I assured my mother that I would come to her if I needed help.

I had altered my classes so I could handle most of my courses online. Travis, being continuously attentive, bought me a brand-new laptop, as well as whatever he thought would keep me happy.

He was as close to perfect as a man could be when it came to taking care of our upcoming child and me. There wasn't a day that went by that my feet weren't rubbed or I was without my rocky road ice cream. Any craving I had, he took care of. Though we lived in separate places, he spent most of his time at my place because I refused to give it up. Some nights, he would stay over, and other nights, he would rub my stomach until I fell asleep and then head to his place.

He was still a gentleman, never pressuring me for physical intimacy, though we had sex more often. The intercourse eventually came to a stop as my belly blossomed, making us both too nervous to continue. It was a welcomed deterrent on my part. In spite of working on being a better girlfriend to him, I still felt there was something missing.

Despite his gentle touches and deep strokes, there was still no fire, at least for me. There was no real passion on my part. I don't know if he was completely oblivious or if he just chose to ignore it.

Though I had claimed to move on, only the thoughts of my passionate nights with J.B. brought me to my orgasms when I was with Travis. When I parted with J.B., I had parted with my fire and passion. Everything else was *still* a substitute.

However, I stayed with Travis because he was so good to me; I still felt a kinship with him. And he was elated about becoming a daddy. He bought baby books in pairs so he could read them while I read them. He knew what to expect when we were expecting. He had even purchased a full-sized cabinet and put it in my bedroom for nothing but nursery items.

He saw to it that I needed nothing.

Well, *almost* nothing.

Deniece was as bad as Travis. She was determined to be my baby's Godmother. On the rare occasions when Travis wasn't with me, she was there to pick up the slack, taking me to doctor's appointments and bringing by ice cream or whatever I craved when she was in the neighborhood.

I admit it. I was spoiled. I don't think I was rotten, but I was definitely spoiled.

As I looked at myself in my pink maternity sundress, I was ready to be spoiled even more for the day. Travis was on his way to pick me up and take me to lunch with my parents, and then to the mall to get the bassinet he had promised me. I was excited and ready to head out for an afternoon with the family.

It had been a couple of weeks since I'd had lunch with my mom, and she was overjoyed to have me and Travis as her guests at the country club where she and my dad were members. I was willing to bet that she was already planning a wedding for us in the back of her mind.

In her opinion, Travis and I were the perfect couple, and she made it known that he would be a welcomed addition to the family. I could only shake my head and roll my eyes at her blatant invitations and suggestions about him becoming a member of the Carter family, as if he would change his name to Carter just for her. It was almost more amusing than it was annoying.

After lunch, we made plans to join my family for dinner the following Sunday. Since I was taking my classes online, I would have more time to spend with them. Sometimes it was a test of patience to be around them. After meeting and getting to know J.B.'s family, I felt like my own were not as relaxed and welcoming to be around. Don't get me wrong, I love my family dearly, but there was just something about being around J.B.'s family that put me at ease. I could be myself around them, not the proper semi-socialite that I was when amongst my family and their friends.

I shook the treasonous thought from my mind while riding in the passenger seat of Travis' car as we headed to the mall. While looking out of the window at the traffic, I couldn't shake the feeling of butterflies in my stomach. I rubbed my belly softly, causing the baby to move slowly. I took Travis' free hand and placed it where our child shifted.

He smiled and tried to keep up with the baby's movement while keeping his eyes on the road. It always made his day to feel the baby move. I was glad to be able to share these small pleasures with him. It was the least I could do.

Once we made it to the mall parking lot, he found a parking space. Always the gentleman, he opened my door for me and helped me out of the car. He walked proudly as I waddled next to him. He was very proud to call me his woman and even more proud to let the world know I was carrying his child. He adored our unborn child and me. I adored him in return.

Minutes after entering the mall, the depth of my adoration was tested.

It had been months since I had seen her. It had been over half a year since she put me out of her place, telling me that I wasn't ready for a relationship with her. It had taken months, chocolate, friends, and a pregnancy for me to finally begin to heal from the hurt of that one night. And all it had taken was seeing her face to face just once to force all of the feelings I had tried to put aside back to the surface.

As if seeing her wasn't enough to shove a knife into my soul, seeing her holding hands with a dime piece who had a "make you drool" body seemed to twist the knife while pushing it deeper.

"Nelle!" she said in genuine surprise.

"Hello, J.B.," I said calmly. "How have you been?"

"I'm makin' it. And you?" she asked with a raised eyebrow.

"I'm doing well," I answered coolly.

For a moment, neither of us spoke. I couldn't stop myself from absorbing her appearance. She looked as gorgeous as ever. She and her companion was a good match.

The thought washed over me like a bucket of ice water. I regained my composure just as Travis cleared his throat.

"I'm sorry," I said quickly. "J.B., you remember Travis, right?"

"How could I forget?" she responded in a polite manner that said so much more than what was stated. She extended her hand to him and they shook. "Congratulations on becoming a daddy," she then said to him.

"Thank you," he replied politely, though I was sure he didn't want to. He then tossed in, "Shay and I love your editorials."

Territory marked.

"I appreciate that," J.B. said with a slick smile, understanding. She then directed our attention to her companion. "Shanelle and Travis, this is my lady, Monique."

Travis shook her hand briefly and then I did the same. Our hands lingered for a moment as we quickly sized each other up.

"Nice to meet you," I said in as friendly of a tone as I could muster.

"The pleasure is mine," she responded, her tone sugary sweet.

Her cell phone rang, and after looking to see who was calling, she excused herself to answer it.

"Probably her agent," J.B. explained as she sashayed away.

"Agent?" I asked, curious.

"Yeah. She's a model," J.B. explained. "She's a real go-getter...knows what she wants out of life. You gotta love that."

The verbal slap to the face.

I had to get away from her.

"Well, it was nice to see you," I said abruptly. "We have to go and get some things for the baby."

"I understand," she responded. "It was nice seeing you, too.

You look happy."

"We are," Travis said, jumping in. "Thanks."

I could only wave quickly before Travis escorted me away to head to the shop to get the bassinet.

Once we were a decent distance away, he asked, "Are you okay?"

"Yeah," I answered after taking a breath.

"Are you sure?" He stopped walking to look me in my eyes.

"Yes," I said with bravado. "I'm good."

He looked at me for another moment before accepting my answer and moving on.

For the rest of the day, I had to keep my feelings in check. Travis was a good man and didn't deserve to see me shook up over an ex. Therefore, I put my best face on and continued my afternoon with him as if nothing had happened. I took extra special care to be attentive and convince him that I was unaffected by seeing J.B.

We enjoyed the day, catching a movie and having dinner before going back to my place. Once we got settled, he put the bassinet together, which made me smile...a real one. Shortly thereafter, I told him that I was tired and ready for bed. We both showered, and he washed my back for me. Once I was dressed for bed, he rubbed my feet as I lay on the pile of pillows he had bought for me. He was the devoted boyfriend and went out of his way to ensure my comfort.

However, as he rubbed my stomach to help me fall asleep, all I could think about was *her*.

The next morning when he kissed me goodbye for the day, all I could think about was *her*. As I laid down for a nap, all I could think of was *her*. And as I touched myself, all I could think about was *her*.

I was consumed by my thoughts of her. I missed her, and in spite of her being in a relationship, I wanted her.

Seeing her brought back as much desire as it did pain. Even

though the civility of our recent interaction bordered on catty, I felt a spark of life that I hadn't felt since we had parted ways. She brought fire into my life just by being in the same room as me.

I ached for her more than ever. Time hadn't healed a thing. Though I was beyond happy about becoming a mother, I still wished I had never walked out of J.B.'s apartment that night.

But, the crime had been committed, and I had been found guilty. I hurt her, and in return, I lost her. She had a new woman, and I had started a family. We had both moved on with our lives.

Over the next couple of weeks, I had to remind myself of that fact on a regular basis. However, each night when I lay in bed, I fell asleep with thoughts of her as Travis rubbed my belly.

I felt a certain amount of guilt each day as I kissed Travis goodbye. Guilt because I knew deep down he wasn't the person that I wanted to be kissing. Guilt because I knew my dependency on him was what had caused my fallout with J.B. in the first place.

My thoughts of J.B. made me feel like I was cheating on him with her, while my heart made me feel like I was cheating on her with him. I was slowly becoming a mess, at least when I was alone. I cried more than ever, but I always had my game face on when around anyone. My emotions were exhausting me, and I didn't know how much longer I could keep up the façade.

I couldn't keep stressing myself, wishing for something that would never be again. The irony was that I realized I was doing the same thing to Travis. I had let him try to push for a relationship that would never be what he really wanted. My heart wasn't in it, and I felt like it was unfair to him. I didn't want him to end up feeling like I had been feeling.

So, I cooked him dinner one night. We ate in what began as a comfortable silence as the radio played in the background. The air seemed heavy in my lungs as I opened my mouth to speak.

"Travis, I got something on my mind that I need to talk to you about..."

That night, I broke up with him. After explaining my reasons why I felt like we didn't belong together, he sat silently for a minute, almost as if the words I spoke had to sink in so he could process them. When he finally opened his mouth, his reaction surprised me.

"Are you fuckin' kidding me right now?" he said, a look of incredulousness written all over his face. "Ever since you told me that you were pregnant, I've done nothing but cater to your ass. I've given you every fuckin' thing."

"I know," I replied sadly. "And I appreciate it all—"

"I don't want your fuckin' appreciation," he interrupted. "I wanted you. Do you really think I was doing this shit just to be a good friend? Hell fuckin' no! I was taking this shit seriously!"

"So was I," I argued back.

"Naw," he said coolly, shaking his head in disagreement. "This was a game for you. You used me as a stand-in since your lil' girlfriend, or whatever the fuck she is, kicked your ass to the curb."

I couldn't stop the hurt that came from those words. " Really?" I began, getting defensive. "You knew what you were getting into when you pursued me. I told you everything!"

"You could've fuckin' said no instead of running around here fuckin' me over and playing house with me like a lil' confused- ass dick-dyke!"

The crack of my palm against his cheek echoed in the room. For a moment, there was no sound. I was shocked at my momentary loss of control. I knew his intention was to hurt me for hurting him, and he had done what he set out to do. In return, out of reflex, I had tried to knock his face off with a slap. A part of me wanted to apologize, but I refused to. He had never talked to me like that, and I knew it was only out of hurt and anger. Still, I wasn't going to let him disrespect me and make me feel like shit in my home.

I watched as he walked wordlessly to the front door and then out of my house. After he slammed the door behind him, I sat in my house alone. There was no tears, only sadness that I had hurt and probably lost someone else who I cared about.

For a week, I heard nothing from him, but I understood. After that week of no contact, he finally began sending text messages to check on me. Finally, he came to see me. He let me know he still intended to be an active father in our child's life, and I was appreciative of that. Though there was some tension between us at first, he also continued to do what he could to help me out. I realized how fortunate I was to have him still willing to be there for me.

I knew he loved me. I loved him, too; just not the way he deserved. But, I was sure we would make things work, even as only friends, for our child's sake.

I had every confidence that he would move on and find the right one for him. The question that nagged me was "Would I?"

Chapter 23
Showers

J.B.

She came to me.

I hadn't realized I had been waiting for her until I laid eyes on her. She looked unsure as I stared at her from my front door. I held out my hand, welcoming her back into my home. After she placed her hand in mine, I gently pulled her close to me.

"What took you so long?" I asked before pulling her closer for a kiss.

Months of being apart hadn't changed the taste of her lips. I got dizzy as I lost myself in the sweetness of her mouth. I didn't want to let her go, but I had to pull away and look at her to make sure she wasn't just an apparition I had created in my mind.

She looked so damn pretty. Her hair had tons of spiral curls but was pulled away from her face with a yellow scarf. Her yellow sundress stopped just above her knee and flowed lightly over her swollen belly. She wore a half-jacket to block the chill of the evening, but I slid it from her shoulders and paid it no attention as it fell to the floor. I continued to stare at her. She smiled shyly. She knew how much I loved her in yellow, and I knew she had worn her clothing just for me.

I smiled.

My beautiful lady had returned to me. She was ready. And I was ready for her.

No words were spoken as I slowly removed the few items she wore. She stood before me naked. She had gained a couple of pounds, but it looked good on her. And the roundness of her belly had me spellbound. Instead of being upset that she was pregnant by a man who wasn't made for her, I was in awe of the fact that she was carrying a new life within her. As she stood before me in her unclothed glory, she was the perfect picture of a young Mother Earth.

I kneeled before her and ran my hand gently across her swollen abdomen, smiling as I felt the small person inside move. I kissed her there before rising to look into her eyes. She turned away, bashful. I turned her back around to face me.

"You are so damn beautiful."

A blush crept across her face, and I couldn't resist kissing her again. She kissed me back shyly at first, but her passion intensified quickly as she wrapped her arms around the back of my neck. We drank from each other as if we had gone without food and water forever. Her kisses nourished my heart and soul.

My hands roamed over her body, caressing every inch of her exposed skin. She whimpered while my fingers slipped into the moisture that had built up between her thighs. As I slowly stroked her clitoris, she gripped my shoulders tightly and whispered my name over and over.

"I got you, baby," I promised, holding her tightly. "I've missed you so much," I whispered before kissing her on the neck.

Unable to resist, I marked her flesh with my mouth so everyone could see that she was mine. There was no Travis to claim her. There was no Monique to claim me. There was only my Nelle and I in the haven of my apartment. The world outside disappeared as it always had when we made love. Nothing else mattered as I took her into my bedroom to lay her down so I could touch and taste her body the way I had so many times before.

I teased her breasts as she groaned and played in my locs. I kissed from her lips to her neck, continuing my trail to the round belly that I had quickly fallen in love with. I continued my journey downward until I was lips-to-lips with her femininity. I parted the soft, succulent flesh and took my first drink from her fountain. She cried out in delight as I got intoxicated from her nectar. I continued to drink and lick her deeply even as she came. I was insatiable, wanting every drop of wetness to flow into my mouth and then throughout my body. I wanted our souls to fuse together from our passion and love for each other...

The bellowing of my alarm yanked me from my state of bliss. I sat up quickly and looked around, and then glanced to my right and found Monique lying next to me. I silenced the alarm, hitting the snooze button for a few more minutes of quiet. I ran my hand across my lips, sure I would find moisture there. Shocked to find none, I realized my mouth and throat were totally dry.

"You okay, baby?" Monique asked sleepily. "Did you have a nightmare?"

"I'm good," I replied. "What made you ask that?"

"You tossed and turned for a while," she answered. "I tried to wake you up, but you weren't havin' it."

"Really?" I asked in feigned surprise.

"Yeah," she answered. "What were you dreaming about?"

After a pause, I responded, "I don't remember."

Yes, it was a blatant lie, but she didn't need to know what was going on in my subconscious. I was still baffled because it had all been a dream. It felt so real that I was convinced I had pussy on my breath.

I could still taste her in my mouth. But, it had only been a dream. A very vivid, realistic motherfucking dream!

I shook my head, trying to clear my mind as I stood up and went to my bathroom. I was wet as hell and horny as fuck, but I didn't want to make love to the woman who was in my bed. To be completely honest, Monique and I had never made love. We had some awesome, wild, uninhibited, off-the-wall sex. I admit that it was good, but it lacked the passion that Shanelle and I had always shared.

I was in need of some passion.

I undressed, stepped into the shower, and turned it on. I needed the shock of the preliminary ice-cold water to cool me off before it warmed up and soothed muscles that were suddenly beyond tense. I scrubbed my skin, trying to wash away the renewed desire I had for my ex. I reminded myself that it had only been a dream and would never be anything more.

By the time I climbed out of the shower and dried off, I could smell bacon and eggs Monique was cooking in the kitchen. Overcome with a new hunger, I quickly brushed my teeth and got dressed so I could meet her at the table for breakfast.

I gave her a quick kiss before sitting down to eat with her.

As we dined, she shared her itinerary with me. She was leaving that morning to do a photo shoot for a men's magazine, and the job had her traveling to Hawaii for the session. She would be gone for a week and wanted to make sure I was aware of her plans. I liked that she felt the need to share her information with me, but in my mind, I really felt like it wasn't a necessary task. Still, I rolled with it.

After eating and straightening up the kitchen, she showered, and then I took her home to gather her belongings for her trip. An hour later, I was seeing her off at the airport with a promise that we would have dinner at a nice restaurant when she got back. I kissed her goodbye and was gone before the plane got off of the ground.

I hit the interstate and headed for the campus to do some work on the newspaper. After making small talk and catching up with some of the staff members, I checked my email.

I came across a message with a subject that simply read

Shanelle Carter. Unable to fight my curiosity, especially after the dream I was still reeling from, I opened the message.

"Baby Shower for Shanelle Carter. This Saturday @ 5 P.M. Be there. And don't you dare come empty handed."

It was signed *D. Ross* and gave the address of where the baby shower would be. I had no idea who D. Ross was, but it did nothing to alter my interest in Nelle's baby shower. After the chilly reunion we had a couple of weeks prior, I wasn't sure I would even be welcomed to such an event. Apparently, *someone* thought I would be. It was tempting, but a part of me figured I should just leave well enough alone. Monique and I had become official, and I didn't want to do anything that would cause us any trouble, especially after sharing my past relationship with Shanelle with her. However, the bigger part of me wanted to see her. I spent the rest of the afternoon debating on what I would do.

Unsure of what decision to make, I called the only person who I felt could help me with this. My mother.

"I think you should go," she said after I explained the situation to her. "You obviously still care about her, so why not?"

"But I have a girlfriend now," I debated. "You don't think it would be unfair to her?"

"If you're that worried about it, tell her about it," my mom said. "What are you afraid of? It's a baby shower at someone's house. It's not like you two are meeting up at a hotel to do the dirty deed—"

"Mama!" I exclaimed, laughing in surprise.

"What?" she said innocently. "I'm just being honest. If it will make you feel better, I will even go to the baby shower with you. I like Shanelle, and I would love to see her again."

"Even though she ripped my heart out and got pregnant just as fast as we could break up?" I challenged.

"I believe the two of you did damage to each other," my mother tossed back at me frankly. "But, I know that girl loved you. I could see it in how she looked at you, and I will always respect and adore her for that. She made a mistake and so did you. Now it's time to be adults and grow from the experience. Maybe seeing her will give you some kind of closure so you can really move on. I'll even go with you to pick out a gift. Just let me know when you wanna go."

Leave it to my mother to be logical.

In her mind, the decision had already been made, but there was still one more person who I felt obliged to consult with. Monique.

"Baby, are you serious?" her voice rose an octave over the phone. "Do you really expect me to be okay with you wanting to go see her?"

"It's not like I'm just wanting to go and see her," I fibbed. "I got an invitation and figured the least I could do was drop her off a gift. We were friends at one point."

"And she is your ex," Monique replied flippantly. I could almost picture her pouting. "I'm gonna be straight up with you. I don't want to sit here worrying about you being alone with her. There was still chemistry. I could see it at the mall when we ran into her."

"Baby," I said, "it's a baby shower. It's not like we're gonna be meeting at a hotel or something. There will be plenty of people. Even my mom will be there—"

"Your mother?" she exclaimed. "I haven't even met your mom yet, but she's gonna go with you to see your ex? And this is supposed to comfort me?"

She had a point.

"I'm sorry, boo," I said lowly. "I didn't think it would be that big of a deal."

"Well, it is," she said, her voice growing calmer, too. "I don't want you to go, *especially* if I'm not there with you."

"Alright," I responded.

I then changed the subject and asked about her day and if she was excited about being in Hawaii. She immediately perked up and started talking my ear off about how beautiful it was and how nice it was to be on an island.

We talked for a few minutes before she told me that she had to go. Honestly, I was relieved to get off the phone. While I appreciated her honesty, I wasn't sure it was going to matter much.

Before I even sat the phone down, I was dialing my mother's number.

"Hello?"

"Hey, Ma," I said. "Where's a good place to get something for a baby shower?"

*****

The huge gift basket contained diapers for newborns, baby wipes, blankets, neutral-colored Onesies, and whatever else my mother could cram into it while making sure it still had a pretty presentation. Wrapped in clear cellophane and tied with a yellow ribbon, it weighed down my arms as my mother and I walked to the front door of the nice house. We had to walk half a block to get to the house because of all the cars parked along the street. It was nearly seven o'clock when we got there since I didn't want to get there too soon or be there too long.

It was a pretty big turnout for her baby shower, and for the first time in a long time, I was nervous to be in a social setting. I didn't want to be under a lot of scrutiny. I knew there would be plenty of people from campus including members of her sorority, and heaven only knew who else. Usually I didn't care who was around, but being in Shanelle's environment instead of my own was something new for me. When we were together, I never got to interact with her in the settings that were second nature to her. So, this made me nervous.

I was so grateful to have my mom beside me to make the situation easier for me to handle. As she rung the doorbell, she rubbed my arm, putting me at ease.

Moments later, the door opened, and I was greeted by a girl who I was sure was one of Shanelle's sorority sisters.

"Come on in," she said with a bright smile. I could hear music coming from another room as she spoke. "I'm Deniece, the hostess. I'm sorry y'all have missed out on most of the games, and she's about done with her gifts, but I'm so glad you could make it!"

She ushered us inside and guided us into the den where we found Shanelle in the process of thanking someone for a gift.

"One more gift!" the hostess interrupted merrily. "Some of y'all already know J.B. Donovan, the editor of the newspaper. And this lovely lady is…"

"Josephine Donovan," my mother filled in with a smile. "I'm J.B.'s mom and future Godmother of the baby."

I heard Nelle's shriek of joy as she awkwardly rose from her chair and made her way over to my mother.

"Mrs. Jo, it is such a surprise!" she said happily. "I am so glad to see you!"

"I'm glad to see you, too, sweetie," my mom said, hugging my ex as if they were long lost friends. She then looked at me. "Well, go set her basket down over there so she can see what we got for the baby."

I did as I was instructed, yet to even say hello to Nelle. I backed away and stood near the entrance of the den as she looked over the contents of the basket. She was positively glowing. She looked so radiant that it didn't bother me when she pulled out each individual item to show everyone.

Needing a moment to myself, I eased into the hallway to gather my thoughts.

"You alright?"

I looked up and found the hostess staring at me.

"I'm good," I answered.

"For a minute, I didn't think you were coming," she said.

After a moment of thinking, I spoke. "So I guess you were the one who sent me the email."

"Ding! Ding! Ding!" she said in amusement. "Very good!"

"Why?" I asked as she walked past me.

"Because she needed to see you," she answered, not breaking her slow stride. "Hungry?"

Baffled, I followed her to the kitchen. "What makes you say that?" I asked, watching her put various finger foods on a Styrofoam plate.

She paused and gave me a look that told me plenty.

"You know?" I asked her, surprised.

"Yeah, I know," she retorted. "It was like pulling teeth, but I finally got it out of her. But, it wasn't like I didn't already know. Personally, I think the two of you just need to get back together, because she's miserable without you."

This new information had my mind spinning.

"Does everyone else know?"

"Nope," she answered. "Just me. Not even her folks."

"Why aren't they here anyway?" I wanted to know.

"They were," she answered. "You missed them by a couple of minutes actually. But, fuck all that. What's up with a reconciliation between you and my soror?"

I was taken aback, yet amused by this woman's bluntness.

"It's not that easy," I answered with a slight laugh.

"What's the problem?" she challenged. "She wants you, and you obviously still feel something for her because you're here."

"Did she tell you she wants me?"

"She doesn't have to," Nelle's friend stated. "I know her."

"I can't go on your assumption, Miss Lady," I told her. "Besides, I have a lady now, and she's with ol' boy. So, it's impossible."

"Nothing is impossible," argued D. Ross with confidence. "And by the way, she and ol' boy aren't together anymore. She broke up with him."

I was officially floored. She'd stumped me. I had no retort for her.

"Mmm hmm. That's right," she said, passing me the plate that she had fixed.

As I reached for a deviled egg, she popped my hand.

"That plate is for your mama. You fix your own."

As she walked out of the kitchen, I could only shake my head. She was feisty, but it seemed like she had a good heart. I'm glad she was there for Nelle.

Nelle. Single. Available. Unattached.

Damn.

I shook the thought as fast as I could create it. I wasn't about to leave the good thing I had simply because Shanelle was single. That was madness.

I made my way back into the den and joined my mom where she sat near Shanelle. I handed her the plate, stealing the deviled egg that I had reached for before. I allowed myself to be comfortable with the room full of women for a little while longer. After all, my mom seemed to be enjoying herself.

After another half hour or so, the crowd began to thin out. Shanelle stood and passed out many hugs and 'thank yous' before she made her way back to my mom and me.

"Thank you for the basket," she said to both of us, though she only looked at me. "I really appreciate it."

"No problem," I told her softly.

I couldn't stop looking at her. I was so aware of her presence that I couldn't think of anything else to say. It was my mother who kept me from going under.

"We had such a nice time, dear," she began, "but it's about

time for us to get on the road before Gerald thinks I've run off to be with another man. He gets so jealous."

Shanelle and I both laughed at her joke, knowing better.

"It was so good to see you," Shanelle said warmly. "I will walk you to the door."

I walked slightly behind the two women as they made plans to do lunch. I watched Shanelle waddle alongside my mother and found the sight adorable. Once we made it to the front door, she hugged my mom and thanked her again for coming. She then turned to me.

"It was really nice to see you again, J.B.," she said almost shyly. "I appreciate the basket so much. You really didn't have to."

"But I wanted to," I told her honestly.

In a surprising moment, she reached out to give me a hug. She felt so good in my arms as I hugged her back.

After releasing her, all I could say was, "Have a good night, Nelle."

"You, too, J.B."

I stood there as she closed the door gently. When I turned around, I found my mom staring at me.

"You two are still in love."

"No, we are not, Mom," I replied as we walked towards the street. "You're reading too much into nothing."

"Yeah right," she scoffed. "I might not know about all of this girl-girl mess, but I know love when I see it."

"You're only seeing it because you want to," I told her.

"The sad thing is you refuse to see it."

"Mama!" I said, frustrated.

"Fine," she said, holding her hands up in surrender. "I won't say anything else about it."

"Thank you," I responded gratefully.

After dropping my mother off at home, I made my way to my place to call my girlfriend. Maybe it was my conscience that had me so anxious to call her.

It seems fate had other plans.

When I got to my apartment, her car was parked in the space next to mine. I smiled as I walked up the steps to my place. She'd come back early, and I was cool with that.

However, the moment I walked into my place, the smile was wiped off of my face.

"What is this?" she said without greeting, holding up the receipt from when I went to buy the items for the gift basket.

"Well, hello to you, too."

"Don't 'hello' me," she said, her irritation obvious. "You went to see her anyway!"

"Look, it was no big deal," I responded.

"No big deal?" she disputed. "It was a big enough deal for you to lie about it!"

She flung the piece of paper at me, and our first argument was given life.

For the next half hour, we went back and forth until we ended up fucking. I learned that arguing turned her on, and I ended up fucking the shit out of her.

As she lay asleep next to me, satiated from our angry sex, all I could think about was Shanelle.

Single.

Chapter 24
Truth and Consequences

Shanelle

I smiled while looking at all of the gifts that took up a corner in my bedroom. I was surprised by how many I had received. More surprising was the visitor who brought the gift basket tied with the yellow ribbon.

I couldn't believe she had come to see me. My heart was racing the entire time she was there. Every time I looked at her, it would skip a beat. It was so hard to keep my cool in front of everyone, but I maintained.

Damn! Why did she have to have such an effect on me after all of this time? I hugged her before she left because I just had to touch her somehow. And oh my God! She smelled so good! It had been over seven months since our breakup, and even after all of that time, I still craved feeling her body near mine.

Would I ever get over her? Had she really ruined me for anyone else?

Even as the thoughts crossed my mind, I could not stop smiling. She had come to see me, and it made me feel good. Even her mother had come. *That* had made me feel special. It was nice to know there were no hard feelings between Mrs. Jo and me. I adored the lady, and she always made me feel comfortable and welcomed.

My smile slipped a little as I wondered where her model chick was. Were they still together? Did the girl not want to come? I could only wonder.

I remembered the day at the mall when I saw her. She looked confident as she shook my hand. I couldn't blame her. She was beautiful. Though I knew I wasn't bad on the eyes by any means, her curves were way more proportionate than mine. Not to mention my round belly did make me feel a little self-conscious and awkward around her. Her walk was sexy, whereas my full-blown waddle had kicked in.

And J.B. seemed proud to be seen with her. Her introduction between us was almost like a "Nanny-nanny-boo-boo, look at what I've got now" session, and her slick comment about her lady "knowing what she wants out of life" was meant to dig at me, and it worked. Ultimately, finally accepting what I really wanted resulted in my breakup with Travis.

I didn't regret the decision. I knew I was being unfair to him and that he deserved someone who really wanted him. As for me, what I wanted was still out of the question, but I was also trying to accept that. Still, I'd rather be alone and on my own than be unhappy while I was with someone. All I could hope for was to fully let go in due time and eventually find someone who could make me feel the way that J.B. had made me feel, or at least close to it. Whether it was a woman or man was irrelevant. I just knew it wasn't Travis.

However, for now, J.B. was still able to create feelings and desires in me that she had no right to do. All it took was for her to enter a room, and I would feel flushed and wanton. I tried to chalk up my feelings to being pregnant and emotional, but I knew better. This woman had touched my soul and left an imprint there. I knew it would be a long time before anyone would even come close to eliciting the feelings she brought out of me. For now, I would just have to be content with the joy that I got from knowing I was going to become a mother. I was okay with that. My baby would need all of my attention anyway.

*****

A couple of weeks went by, and during that time, I had to make myself keep from trying to contact her. I knew I had no right to. Despite my breakup with Travis, I was still spending time with him. He even continued to join me for dinners with my parents. Never did I expect my involvement with him to lead into my first fallout with my family.

The irony of the situation was that the argument started because he *wasn't* with me. It happened one evening when I came to dinner without him.

"I'm surprised Travis let you come without him," my mom said as we sat in the den letting our dinner settle.

"Travis has a life outside of being with me," I replied.

"I can't tell," my mom half-joked. "But, there's nothing wrong with that. He adores you, and he's good to you. He's going to make a good husband for you in the future."

"Mom," I began, "please don't start."

I wasn't up to dealing with the marriage talk at the moment.

"What?" she said innocently. "It's true. I'm surprised he hasn't popped the question already, what with you carrying his child and whatnot."

"Well, I don't see him popping anything with me," I said honestly.

"Well, why not?" my mother exclaimed as if she had just been insulted. "You are one of the best catches in town. You're beautiful, smart—"

"Mother," I interrupted, "it has nothing to do with me being a good catch or whatever."

"You two look so good together," she continued as if I weren't trying to speak. "Are you giving him a hard time? What's the problem?"

"He's just not who I envision spending my life with, Mom."

"Then why are you involved with him?" she sputtered. "Apparently, there's something there, dear."

"Yes, there is," I agreed, pointing to my stomach.

"Shanelle!" she exclaimed in shock. "Seriously?"

"Please don't get all dramatic on me, Mother," I said before I could stop myself.

I had never been disrespectful to my parents, and I never raised my voice in their home, but my mother was getting to me. I took a deep breath to calm my nerves and then I spoke.

"I didn't want to say anything, but I guess it's time to let you know. Travis and I aren't together anymore, and we haven't been for weeks."

"What?" my mother said in surprise. "What happened?"

"Irreconcilable differences," I answered slickly. When my mother stared at me wordlessly, I added, "He's just not the one for me."

"Well, how do you know?" my mom interrogated. "Did you even give him a chance?"

"Yes, I did," I replied. "But, it wasn't working for me, and I didn't want to ruin the friendship we already had."

"It wasn't working for you?" she mocked. "It worked enough for you to get pregnant with his child."

I was taken aback by my mother's vehemence. "Mom!"

After a moment, she said, "I'm sorry, my darling, but I just had such high hopes for the two of you."

"I know," I responded softly. "I just couldn't continue to be with someone who I wasn't in love with. It wasn't fair to either of us."

My mother sighed. "I guess you make sense."

I had considered it a small victory on my part. My mother was never wrong, at least in her eyes.

"So is there someone else in your life?"

I don't know why I didn't see that question coming.

"There was," I answered carefully, "but that is also in the past."

"Anyone we know?" she asked, her interest ignited.

"I doubt it," I replied slowly, praying she would drop the subject. I should've known better, though.

"Well, tell us about him," she requested. "Your dad and I would love to know about him."

I looked at my dad, who had been quiet the whole time reading his newspaper. He looked for a moment, waited, and then returned his attention to his paper.

"There's really not much to tell," I said hesitantly. "It didn't work out, so it's irrelevant."

"Well, why didn't it?" my mother pried.

"Because I wasn't ready to give them what they wanted from me," I answered cryptically.

"And what was that?"

Why did she have to be so nosy?

"It's a long story, Mom," I said with a sigh. I rubbed on my belly to bring myself comfort. It had become a habit. "I really don't want to go into it right now."

But my mom being the way she was, refused to stop digging.

"So *he* must have broken it off with *you*."

In a moment of irritation, I responded, "No, Mother. *She* broke it off with me."

For a moment, I think the air stopped circulating in the room as my comment registered with both of my parents.

"What in the hell—" my father began, but he was cut off by my mother.

"You can't be serious!" she yelled. "Tell me you're joking!"

"No, ma'am. I'm not joking."

"I don't understand," she said, shaking her head. "*She* as in one of those lesbians? Have you lost your mind?" She then turned to my dad and said, "Make sure we set her up an appointment with Dr. Smith tomorrow. We can't have her passing anything on to our grandchild."

It was then that I lost my cool.

"What the fuck do you mean?" I sprang up as fast as my round body would allow me. "Pass something on to the baby? Are you fuckin' serious right now?"

"Don't you dare talk to me like that!" my mother demanded. "Do you know what those types of women do? They carry diseases from their nasty sexual escapades—"

"How would you know?" I interrupted, thoroughly insulted. "You are too well educated to say some dumb shit like that, Mother."

"Dale!" she yelled at my father. "Are you just going to keep letting her disrespect me like this in our home?"

"What are you gonna do, Mother?" I challenged. "Put me out?"

She turned her back on me and didn't say another word.

My father looked at me as if he had never seen me before, his shock still evident in his voice when he finally spoke again.

"I think it might be best if you just go."

My jaw dropped, but only for a brief moment. While gathering my purse and jacket, I told them, "Fine."

However, before I left, I had one more thing to say.

"I didn't want you to find out like this, and I hate that it went this way. I was afraid to tell you because I was afraid of how you'd react. I mean, I knew you wouldn't be thrilled about it, but what I didn't expect was such rejection and downright ignorance from the two of you."

And with that, I was gone.

I waddled my way out of the door and to my car, and drove myself home. Even though I tried my hardest to hold back the tears, they came. They streamed down my cheeks as I drove to my apartment, and they continued as I called Deniece and told her what happened. I cried when she brought me rocky road ice cream and ate half a gallon with me. I could not stop crying.

I was in shock. I was hurt. I was pissed!

As I lay in bed that night with swollen eyes, I felt a sense of relief in spite of the hurt. I had taken a big step, coming out to my parents. It didn't go at all how I would've liked, but a weight had been lifted from my shoulders.

Weeks went by without an exchange between my parents and me. It pained me not to share baby news and other things with them, but I refused to beg them to communicate with me, especially with my mother's distorted view of what it meant for two women to be together.

I wish I could've told them how happy this one woman had made me and how good she was to me. I wished I could've told them that she was everything to me that they wanted Travis to be, and then some. But, I was never given the chance, and my pregnancy-induced temper had gotten the best of me, causing me to speak to my mother in ways I never had before.

A part of me wanted to apologize because I know what I had said to her was disrespectful. I had never been disrespectful, always wanting to be the perfect daughter. I had reacted out of shock and anger, and I knew I had hurt my mother, but hell, she had hurt me, too. I felt like she owed me an apology, as well.

I was shocked at how misinformed she was about lesbianism. I was still rather new to the game, but I knew her perception was faulty.

Then again, could I call myself a lesbian? After all, I had laid up and made a baby with a man after a breakup with the woman I loved. I then proceeded to try to have a relationship and build a family with this guy. Did I love him? Yes. Did I want to be his woman? No.

I couldn't be with him because I was in love with a woman. I still loved J.B., but did the fact that I loved her make me a true lesbian? I'm sure my circumstance would be up for debate in the gay community. Maybe I was just a woman who happened to fall in love with another woman.

Whatever I was, I knew my mother was wrong, and until she was ready to admit it and get past her prejudices, she wouldn't have to worry about hearing from me. My child and I would be just fine, with or without her.

Travis told me that I was being stubborn, and I admit he was right. Nevertheless, I wasn't going to change my stance or my decision.

The day before Thanksgiving, he nearly begged me to call my family. He was going out of town for the holiday, and he didn't want me to be alone. I assured him that I would be fine and that I was having dinner with Deniece and her family. He still wasn't convinced.

"I could just stay here with you," he suggested when he came by to check on me before his flight.

"No, go enjoy yourself. Eat tur-duck-en. Get fat."

"You know I'm going to worry about you," he said. "I wish you could come with me."

"You know I'm too far along to travel," I told him with a smile.

"That's exactly why I should stay with you."

"Nope," I said, nudging him towards the door. "I refuse to let you miss out on this trip. The ticket is paid for, and you're going. By this time tomorrow, I will be at Niecy's eating, just like you."

After ten more minutes of debating, he finally gave in. I gave him a hug and a kiss on his cheek and told him to enjoy himself. Later that evening, Deniece came by and checked on me.

"You wanna go to this Thanksgiving party with me tonight?" she asked as I reclined on my sofa.

"The only party I'm going to is being hosted by this sofa," I answered with a laugh.

"Awe," she said, pouting as she kneeled next to me to rub my belly. "You and my niece don't wanna shake y'all booties a little bit?"

"No, we don't," I responded, unable to hold back a smile. "And what makes you so sure the baby is a girl?"

"Because I want her to be," she answered simply. "I don't know why you wanted to do the whole 'I don't wanna know' bit. You should've let your doctor tell you so I could go ahead and buy her the A.K.A. pajamas."

I laughed at my friend, and we talked for a few more minutes before she headed out.

Other than when I made several runs to the bathroom, I was a couch potato. Before I knew it, I had fallen asleep. I awakened around one in the morning to my phone ringing.

"Hello?"

"Hey, girl!" Deniece said. "I am so tipsy!"

Though sleepy, I laughed. "You sound like it. You better not be driving."

"No!" she said. "I'm riding with Shayla, and I'm almost home. I just wanted to check on you."

"I'm good, girl. Get home safely. I'll see you tomorrow."

After hanging up with her, I turned awkwardly to my side and fell back asleep.

What seemed like moments later, a shooting pain ripped me out of my sleep. I immediately got up from the sofa. I rubbed my lower abdomen, and the pain gradually subsided. I then headed to the kitchen to get something to drink.

Before I could make it to the cabinet for a glass, I was hit again with a wave of pain that nearly knocked me on my butt. Then came that telltale trickling down my leg. I was stuck where I stood for a few moments, rubbing my belly and praying for the pain to go away.

"Really?" I said aloud. I looked at my stomach and spoke to the child who apparently was ready to make their entrance into the world. "You couldn't wait one more week, huh?"

As if responding, another contraction came quickly and hard.

"Holy shit!" I said, catching my breath.

I tried to remember my breathing techniques as I made my way back into the living room. I picked up my phone and dialed Deniece's number to no avail.

"Damn," I muttered.

I'm sure she was in an alcohol-induced slumber. I paced for a minute, hesitant to dial the next number.

"You've reached the Carter residence. Sorry we can't come to the phone..."

I hung up in frustration as another contraction hit me. I redialed my parents' number and left a message.

"Mom, Dad. I know we aren't speaking, but um, I kinda went into labor, and I would really like for you to be a part of this. Please call me back whenever you get this message. I love you guys."

I was able to get Travis on the phone. He answered on the first ring.

"What's wrong?" was his greeting.

"Hi," I said with a shaky voice. "I just thought I would let you know that I'm about to head to the hospital. I think I'm in labor."

"I knew I should've stayed!" he exclaimed. "Are you okay?"

"I'm good," I answered. "Just a little nervous."

"Who's taking you?" he asked anxiously.

"I can't get in touch with anyone," I answered. "I'm just gonna call 911."

He cursed a blue streak. "I will be on the first thing smoking," he told me. "Call me and let me know as soon as the ambulance gets there."

"Okay," I told him before he assured me that he would be back as soon as possible.

After we ended our call, I pressed 9-1-1, but something kept me from pressing the 'send' button. I was terrified, and I didn't want to go alone. I paced through several contractions before working up the nerve to call her. She answered the phone after three rings.

"Hello?" she said groggily.

"J.B.," I said weakly as I tried to talk through a contraction. "I need you."

Chapter 25
New Life

J.B.

"J.B., I need you."

I sat up abruptly. I had reacted out of reflex when I answered my cell phone. Until I heard her voice, I hadn't even realized it was her ringtone that played on my phone.

"Nelle?" I said, momentarily confused.

I rubbed my eyes and ran my hand down my face to make sure I wasn't dreaming…this time.

"I'm sorry to call you so late," she said, sounding anxious and in a rush, "but Travis is out of town and Nieci is drunk and me and my parents aren't talking—"

"Whoa-whoa-whoa," I interrupted, getting out of my bed. "Slow down, baby girl."

"Baby, who is that?" Monique said sleepily from behind me.

I barely heard her as I walked out of my bedroom and into the living room, where I sat on the edge of my sofa.

"Now," I said calmly, though my nerves were already on alert. For Shanelle to call me, it had to be serious. "What's wrong?"

"My water broke," she said, panic in her voice. "I didn't have anyone else to call, and I don't want to go alone. I'm scared, J.B."

"Don't be," I told her, jumping to my feet. "I'll be there in a few minutes."

I quickly disconnected the call and headed towards my bedroom. Once I flipped on the light, I saw Monique sitting on the bed staring at me.

"Where are you going?" she asked, though I figured she already knew.

"Shanelle's in labor," I explained while throwing on a pair of sweat pants. I then rummaged through my closet for the matching sweater.

"And what does that have to do with you?" Monique demanded, folding her arms across her chest.

"She said she doesn't have anyone else to call." I sat on the bed to put some tennis shoes on.

"And you believe that shit?" my mate challenged. "She just wants you to be there!"

"If she's bullshittin', I'll be right back," I said nonchalantly.

"Your ex having a baby is not your problem," Monique fussed as I stood up.

"I'm not about to do this with you right now," I said, turning around to look at her briefly. "I'm not gonna just leave her hangin'."

"Like she did you?" she taunted, standing up and putting her hand on her hip.

"Now that was fucked up," I told her with a humorless laugh. "Are you jealous of her or something, Miss Model?"

"Hell no!" she answered with vehemence. "I have you," she said confidently.

"Are you sure about that?"

Her response was shocked silence, and I laughed again.

"Go back to sleep, Monique."

I turned the light off to my bedroom as if she wasn't standing there.

"I might not be here when you get back," she threatened softly.

"Well, if you leave, don't fuck with my shit," I warned her.

I walked out of my front door and locked it from the outside.

I didn't have time for the fussing and fighting. Her threat to leave didn't daunt me. I chuckled about it as I pulled out of my parking space. If she wanted to leave, then so be it. I wasn't about to chase or baby her because she wanted to throw a temper tantrum.

There was something, or better yet someone very important at stake, and whether or not she wanted to be waiting for me when I got back made no difference to me. I cared for her, but if she thought threatening me was going to make a difference, she had life all mixed up.

My thoughts of Monique and her pouting evaporated as I pulled up to Shanelle's apartment. I quickly made my way to the door and beat on it fretfully.

When she whipped the door open, I could see the pain on her face.

"You okay?"

If looks could kill, I would've hit the ground from the look she gave me.

"My bad," I said, holding my hands up in surrender. "Ready?"

"I need my bags," she said, pointing to a duffle bag and a baby bag on her couch.

I moved to them quickly and wasted no time getting back to her. "Let's go."

I turned off the lights and locked her front door before helping her down the steps. I held her hand while guiding her to my car. After opening the door for her and making sure she was secured, I made my way to the driver's side, tripping as I passed the front bumper. Her giggle as I got into my seat assured me that she had seen the stumble.

"Are you okay?" she asked with a laugh before focusing on her breathing.

"I'm good," I answered, wondering when my nerves had

kicked in.

"Good, because we can't both be in the hospital tonight. I need you by my side, not in the emergency room."

After driving for a little while, I turned off my radio.

"Why didn't you have anyone else to call?" I wanted to know.

"Travis is out of town, and Deniece went out and got buzzed," she replied.

"Why did he leave knowing you could pop any day now?" I asked, irritated with her baby's daddy. Or maybe it was just the fact that I didn't care much for him in general.

"Well," she began, "I'm not due for another few weeks, so this is a surprise for us both."

"And where are your parents?" I probed.

"We haven't been on good terms for a little while," she answered with sadness in her voice.

"What happened?"

"I told them about you."

For a minute, I was rendered speechless. I didn't know what to say. There was so much more that I wanted to know, but I didn't have the opportunity to ask. I pulled up to the front of the emergency room entrance. I parked in the 'No Parking' zone, ran into the building, and approached the front desk anxiously.

"Can I help you?" the woman asked nicely.

"My girl is having a baby," I answered, feeling excitement build up within my body. "She can barely get around from the contractions."

Within a minute or two, Shanelle was in a wheelchair being pushed inside while I found a parking space.

My feet couldn't move fast enough as I made my way back to the hospital entrance. When I got inside, they were taking her towards another door. I was about to take a seat in the waiting room, when she called my name.

"What are you doing?" she asked as I hurried over to her.

"About to sit down," I answered simply.

"I want you with me," she said, grabbing the hem of my sweater.

"You mean, while you push—"

"Yes!" she shrieked in a mix of frustration and pain.

I hadn't prepared to actually be *in* the delivery room with Nelle, but as I looked in her eyes, I knew there was no way I could tell her no. As they prepped her, they prepped me, as well, making sure my clothing was covered and I was as sanitized as possible.

While standing next her, I looked at her face, which was calm in some moments and then contorted in pain the next. Her breathing was labored, and her discomfort was apparent, but she handled it like a trooper.

I only half heard what was going on around me. The words "no time for an epidural" and "fully dilated" went in one ear and out the other. I had zoned out for a few minutes, seeing only her face. I had no clue as to what was going on until I heard the doctor telling her that it was time to push.

I snapped out of my semi-trance and focused. I wanted to help her, but I was clueless. I looked at one of the nurses.

"What do I do?" I asked.

"Just try to keep her calm and—"

"Bitch, I am calm!" Nelle interrupted venomously.

"Nelle!"

The look she gave me was enough to kill my fussing. Fortunately, the nurse didn't appear to be bothered by her outburst. I'm sure she was probably used to it.

She then looked at the nurse, almost sad. "I'm so sorry," she said meekly.

I thought she was going to cry for a minute, but the anger sharks quickly started swimming again as she had another contraction.

"I am never doing this shit again!" she yelled.

"I need you to push, Shanelle," the doctor ordered. "Push."

She tried weakly.

"It hurts," she cried. Beads of sweat trailed down her face.

I looked around. As if reading my mind, the nurse nodded her head towards the nearby table.

I took a cool wet towel and dabbed the sweat from Nelle's forehead. In spite of her pain, she gave me a look of gratitude.

I continued to wipe the perspiration from her head as the doctor kept telling her when to push. It pained me to see her in such pain. The more I watched her, the more I was convinced I would never give birth.

"I can't do this," she said, trying to readjust herself.

The nurse immediately stopped her, catching her by her shoulders.

"You can do it," her doctor urged. "You're almost there. The baby is crowning. I am looking at the head. You just have to push."

"You can do it, baby girl," I repeated.

Wordlessly, she grabbed my hand and squeezed it tightly as she pushed again.

"That was a good one," the doctor cheered. "Give me one more good push," he instructed.

"I can't," she cried. "I'm so tired!"

"Come on, baby girl," I cajoled her. "Push, baby. You can do it. Just hold my hand and push. One more time."

The scream that escaped from her throat as she pushed could be compared to the roar of a lion.

For a moment, there was silence. Then a small but strong cry was heard in the room.

I released a breath that I hadn't realized I was holding.

"Congratulations!" the doctor told her. "You are the mother of a beautiful baby girl."

Shortly thereafter, I watched as Shanelle cried tears of joy and held her daughter in her arms.

"She's gorgeous," she said in awe.

"Just like her mother," I stated to her softly.

She smiled up at me and readjusted the tiny bundle so I could see her better.

"Thank you so much, J.B."

"No need to thank me," I told her modestly, and I meant it.

It was an honor for me to be a part of such a major event. I was even given the honor of cutting the umbilical cord. It meant more to me than I could ever begin to describe.

"What's her name?" I asked while looking at the darling baby girl.

"Mikayla," she answered. "Mikayla Brianna Carter."

For a moment, I was speechless, surprised.

"Really?" I asked in wonder.

She nodded and smiled at me. "You like it?" she asked shyly.

"I love it," I answered, feeling a lump grow in my throat. I tried to clear my throat, swallow, but nothing helped. I excused myself, claiming the need to go to the bathroom. I made it out to the hallway before a tear slipped from my eye.

I was overwhelmed by the feeling that came over me. I had never experienced such a beautiful moment in my life, and to make it even more special, she had given her daughter my middle name. I was beyond touched by the gesture.

After regaining my poise, I went back into the room. I sat with her for a few more minutes, making sure she was okay before telling her that I would be back in a few hours to see her and the baby. After giving her a kiss on the forehead, I left her to rest and made my way home.

I pulled into my parking space and noticed that Monique's car was gone. I was actually grateful for her absence. I wanted to get a few hours of rest, then go back to see Nelle and Mikayla without having to argue with my girlfriend.

I skipped up the steps to my apartment and let myself in. The note on my dining room table immediately caught my attention. I read it slowly, waiting for a sense of loss that never came. The 'Dear John' letter was simple and to the point. She wasn't willing to compete with my ex, and I couldn't blame her for that. Monique and I had some very nice times together, and I hoped maybe we could at least be cordial in the future. In that moment, thought, it really didn't bother me as much as it probably should have that she had left. I shook off the whole issue and made my way to my bedroom.

My mood quickly changed when I saw the appearance of my room. It had been destroyed. My sheets had been ripped to shreds as well as some of my clothes. My flat screen television lay face down on the floor. After sitting it upright, I realized it had been torn up. I straightened the mattress that had been pulled halfway off the box spring. When I looked at the mirror on my dresser, I saw the other note she had written in red lipstick: "FUCK YOU, BITCH!"

It took me nearly an hour to get my room back together. As I cleaned, I promised myself that I would make sure to cross her path again. At the same time, I thought about the bullet I had dodged with her. I reminded myself to get my locks changed as I took a bag of my torn clothes to the trash bin outside. I exorcised her from my mind after putting fresh sheets on the bed and lying down.

I could barely sleep. I tossed and turned from my anxiousness. After failing at my attempts to rest, I took a shower and fixed myself a quick breakfast. I could hardly taste my eggs as I munched. I was so anxious to get back to Nelle and Kayla.

By nine-thirty, I was heading to Nelle's room with my arms and hands filled with flowers, balloons, and a stuffed animal. I was not ready for what awaited me.

The chatter that had been going on when I entered the room immediately stopped. I knew the people who were standing over the hospital-provided bassinet were Nelle's parents. For a long moment, nothing was said. It was Shanelle who finally broke the silence.

"Back so soon?" she asked, sounding happy.

The smile on her face and in her voice was genuine, and it warmed me from the inside out, fighting the frostiness that I felt coming mainly from her mother.

"I couldn't stay away," I told her honestly. "I am already in love with that little girl."

"I don't blame you for that," she said as I put her arrangements from the gift shop on the corner table. She then spoke to her parents. "Mom, Dad, this is a very close friend of mine, J.B. Donovan." She then looked at me and said, "J.B., these are my parents."

"It's nice to meet you," I said, extending my hand in greeting.

Mr. Carter accepted my hand in a polite handshake. Mrs. Carter, on the other hand, refused to acknowledge my extended hand and gave me a look that bordered on disdain. *Stuck-up bitch*, I wanted to shout. Quickly taking reign of my temper, I returned my attention to Nelle.

"I just wanted to drop off this stuff. I hope you like them."

"I do," she said with an apologetic smile. "You don't have to go," she told me.

I looked at her mother and had to catch myself again.

"Trust me, I do."

"I understand," she said before cutting a quick, dirty look at her maternal figure. "Will you come back later?"

"Only if you want me to," I answered, feeling the tension thicken in the room.

"Yes, I definitely do."

"Then I will," I told her, unable to resist smiling at her despite the situation.

In a move to purposely add fuel to the fire, I walked over to her and gave her another kiss on her forehead. She didn't seem to mind, but I heard her mother's intake of breath, and I admit it brought me pleasure.

I smiled as I left the hospital room. I smiled all the way to the elevator. However, the smile fell from my face once the elevator door opened.

"Hello, J.B."

"Hello, Travis."

For a moment, we just looked at each other. The silence was a little awkward, but he killed it, subsequently killing my mood, as well.

"It was nice to see you," he said with a slick smile. "I'm going to meet my daughter for the first time."

"Congratulations," I said solemnly.

"Thank you," he responded, still smiling as he walked away proudly.

The quick exchange with Travis and the icy meeting with Shanelle's parents dampened my mood for a good part of the afternoon. However, receiving a call from her letting me know that she was looking forward to seeing me later made me feel a little better.

That evening when I went to see her, she apologized for how her mother acted and told me that she was glad I came back to see her and the baby. As I sat in the chair next to the baby, I was given the opportunity to hold Kayla. As I looked at her tiny face, I fell head over heels in love with her. As I looked up at her mother, I accepted that I had never fallen *out* of love with her.

I wanted them both in my life.

How could it work, though? It was obvious her mother had distaste for me, and I wasn't about to kiss her ass just because she was Shanelle's mom or because she was a Carter. I couldn't figure out her father yet. He seemed like the quiet type, but that meant nothing. In spite of coming from old money, he acquired his wealth on his own, and I knew he didn't do it by being a sheep. And then there was Travis. He and I were never going to be buddies, but I knew he was going to always be in Nelle's life.

I knew there were going to be some hurdles involved with trying to reconcile with Shanelle. I had never wanted to get back with an ex, so I didn't know how to go about making it happen. But, I was willing to try.

My love for Shanelle had been renewed the moment my namesake had taken her first breath. I wanted my Nelle back, and I wanted us to work it out.

The question was: How could I let *her* know that?

Chapter 26
So Good

Shanelle

Three months had passed since I had given birth to Kayla. It had been three months of change for me. I was more than just a college student or a member of a sorority or someone's daughter. I was now a mother. In such a short time, I had matured a lot. I learned what it meant to be responsible for someone else's life, and I took that job very seriously.

Even after three months, I was still getting used to having a baby attached to my nipples at regular intervals, but I had no complaints. I had a beautiful, healthy, happy daughter on my hands, so the breastfeeding wasn't a big issue for me.

I was in a happy place. I had Kayla in my life. Between Travis, my family, and me, she was well loved and well taken care of. Deniece was already spoiling her and immediately claimed the position of Godmother. The icing on the cake was the fact that J.B. had also filled the position.

Yes, J.B. had returned to my life on a regular basis, though we were just friends. From the day that Kayla was born, J.B. had become a constant force in my life. She was in love with my daughter, and it made me very happy to know that.

My only issue was the fact that *I* was still in love with *her*. It was a challenge to keep my feelings to myself and keep it platonic, but I was so glad she was in my life that I continued to torment myself by keeping her around. To my delight, we were slowly getting to know each other again. She had become such a good friend, and I cherished that.

However, my desire for her continued to simmer at the very depths of my soul. I spent many late nights with Kayla sleeping in her bassinet just outside my bedroom door because I felt some kind of way about her being in the room with me while I played with myself, even in the dark. I wanted J.B. with a passion that surpassed anything I had ever felt before.

I knew her touch, her taste, her stroke. It was all embedded in my memory. I wanted no one's touch but hers. I was truly scarred and ruined for anyone else.

It made me wonder if soul mates really did exist. On the other hand, in order for us to be soul mates, we would both have to feel the same way, and I wasn't sure we did. She was as sweet as ever, polite, and so good to Kayla, but that didn't mean she felt the way that she once did for me.

Even if there was a small chance she did, there was still an obstacle that would make things hard for us. My parents. Better yet, I'm going to say my mother. In the few rare moments that she and J.B. were in the same room, she was civil but still cold. Even when I told her that nothing was going on between J.B. and I, she still held on to that attitude of hers.

My association with J.B. put a strain on my relationship with my mother, but it had gotten to the point where it didn't matter much to me. I had already told my mother if she couldn't accept me for who I was and what I did with my life, she could just as easily walk out the door. I knew she wouldn't because her granddaughter had stolen her heart, as well. So, she would endure whatever she had to in order to keep spoiling her grandbaby.

As far as my father, he was neutral about the whole thing. Or at least, if he felt some kind of way about it, he kept his opinion to himself. I was grateful for that.

It seemed like the only person who was pushing for me to take my relationship with J.B. to the next level was Deniece. She took every opportunity she could to remind me that we were both single.

"So are you," I reminded her one afternoon while we were at the mall.

"For the most part, that's true," she said, "but it's by choice and at least I *am* dating. You, on the other hand, are in love."

"J.B. and I are friends," I responded while slowly pushing the stroller containing my sleeping baby. "I am perfectly okay with our friendship."

"You are perfectly full of shit," she said with a laugh. "What are you afraid of? Y'all have been dancing around each other for months, bein' all friendly and stuff, knowing that you want her to knock the dust off that pus—"

"Nieci!" I interjected, laughing hard. "When did you become such a potty mouth?"

"Don't try to change the subject, girl. Y'all could at least be making sex faces. I know you haven't been getting any because you barely have a life since you had my Godbaby. Haven't you ever heard of friends with benefits?"

"I don't want just benefits. And besides, I'm happy with being with my baby," I debated.

"But Kayla can't scratch that itch, girl!"

I laughed harder. "Let me worry about my itch, okay?"

"Whatever you say," she replied, throwing her hands up in surrender. "I'm dropping it."

I continued to laugh, knowing she would be at it again before long.

We finished walking around the mall and headed back to my place.

After we got home, I went to change Kayla's diaper. I took her and lay her on the comforter on my bed. As soon as I started cleaning her, my cell phone rang in the living room. Recognizing J.B.'s ringtone, I yelled for Deniece to bring my phone to me. But, it seems she had other plans.

"Well, hello, J.B.," I heard her say in the living room. "She's changing Kayla. How are you?" There was a brief pause before she continued. "We were probably just gonna watch a movie or something. Hey, I have a great idea!" she continued with excitement in her voice. "My girl hasn't had a real night out since she had the baby," she began.

"Nieci!" I said in a warning tone.

She continued as though I hadn't spoken. "Why don't you take her to a movie or out to eat or something while I babysit so she can have a couple of hours off of mommy duty?" Pause. "Perfect! She'll be ready by seven! Okay! See you then!"

I released a breath that I didn't realize I was holding. "Nieci, I'm going to kill you!"

She walked to my doorway and smiled as she leaned against my door jam. "No, you're not," she said confidently. "Don't try to act like you're not excited."

I turned and finished redressing my baby, hiding the smile that crept across my lips. After tossing the diaper in the Diaper Genie, I picked Kayla up and walked past my smiling friend.

"Okay, so where are we going, Cupid?"

"She's going to take you to eat and catch a movie," she answered. "I will take good care of Kayla. You just try to have a good time tonight. If you're not going to get any nookie, at least take a couple of hours to enjoy yourself with the person you want the nookie from."

"You're silly," I told my friend.

I couldn't even pretend to be mad. Nieci was such a busybody and always in my business, but I admit I was actually grateful. Even though I said I was happy with spending all of my free time with Kayla, I really did need a small break, and I couldn't think of anyone better to spend the time with than J.B. When I refused to take that step of trying to spend time with J.B., my best friend took it for me.

I was ready and waiting by quarter to seven.

Though I tried to seem blasé about it, I was very excited about my outing with J.B. I was as excited about this outing as I was about our first date. I went through my closet, rejecting tons of clothing combinations before settling on a black sweater dress that hugged my curves from my shoulders to just above my knees. Though I was ten pounds heavier than I had been before my pregnancy, I was still happy with my figure, and the dress emphasized my silhouette. A pair of black high-heeled boots and some silver accessories finished my look. I used my curling iron to give my hair soft curls and applied light make-up. I looked at my reflection in the mirror, and I approved. Just to be sure, I got a second opinion from Deniece.

"How do I look?" I asked her.

"You look so cute for your date," she gushed, giving me the thumbs-up.

"It's not a date," I told her, unable to fight the smile that crept onto my face.

"Then why are you so giddy?"

Before I could come up with a witty reply, my doorbell rang, announcing J.B.'s arrival. Instantly, butterflies began to flutter in my stomach, making me feel like a teenager going on her first date. However, when I opened the door, my body's response reminded me that I was a grown woman.

As J.B. stood in front of me, dressed casually in tan slacks and a tan and blue sweater vest, my libido caught on fire. Her hair had been freshly twisted, and though she had it tied back, it fell several inches further down her back than it had when we first went out. The diamonds in her earlobes seemed to sparkle more brightly than they usually did. I remembered how soft her lips were as I snuck a quick peek at them when she smiled at me.

"Good evening," she said with a smile that bordered on seductive.

The desire to reach out and touch her was almost overwhelming.

"Hello to you," I said, feeling my cheeks grow warm as she gave me a slow once over.

I felt naked under her gaze, and the look in her eyes said she approved of what she saw. I smiled in delight as she presented me with a long-stemmed pink rose.

"Thank you," I said, my joy in her gesture evident in my smile.

"Ready to go?" she asked, still hitting me with those piercing eyes of hers.

"Yes," I answered. I went and gave Kayla a kiss and told Nieci, "Take good care of my baby."

"I've got this," Deniece replied confidently. "Go and enjoy yourself, hopefully a lot."

"Hush," I said with a laugh.

The look on J.B.'s face let me know she had also heard my friend. "I will take good care of her," she informed my friend with a wink.

"Oh, I believe you will!" she said back, her comment dripping with innuendo.

I grabbed my purse and ushered J.B. out of the door before Deniece could say anything else that might embarrass me.

The ride to the movie theater was comfortable. We listened to some R&B, made small talk, and decided on a movie based on another comic book. After getting our tickets, we stopped by the snack bar for some Twizzlers, popcorn, and drinks. Shortly thereafter, we were in our seats waiting for the lights to go down and the movie to start.

"I've wanted to see this movie for a while," I said while ripping open the strawberry-flavored candy. After taking a bite of a flimsy stick, I added, "I heard it was a good movie."

"Me, too," J.B. said, making herself more comfortable in her seat. "I'm glad we came in the middle of the week. It's not that many people in here."

"I'm glad, too," I agreed as the lights went down.

The first half of the movie went by quickly. We snacked and made small comments about the movie while enjoying each other's company. It wasn't until her leg touched mine that my body became aware of her presence again. It was the most innocent of touches, but the feeling of her body so close to mine had my nerves standing at attention. She seemed oblivious to the contact, so I tried to calm myself down. *We're just friends and nothing more*, I reminded myself in my head over and over again. I returned my attention to the movie and bit into my last licorice stick.

"Can I get one of those?" she leaned over and whispered to me.

"I'm sorry," I told her. "This is my last one." I wagged it at her playfully.

"Oh, so you're just gonna tease me with it, huh?" she said with a laugh, watching me take another bite.

'Ooh, and it's so good, too," I bragged as I held up the last morsel of the candy. "Want it?" I teased, waving it in her face.

Catching me off guard, she caught my hand. She then took the candy from my fingers with her lips, allowing her tongue to graze my fingertips in the process. The smile on her face was one of victory, and I was temporarily rendered speechless.

"You want it back?" she teased seductively.

"You make me sick," I said in mock irritation. She only laughed. "I gotta pee," I said abruptly.

I rose from my seat and quickly crossed in front of her to make my way to the ladies' room. I had to get away for a minute. I paced in the bathroom for a moment before going into a stall for a minute of real privacy. I was soaking wet!

It had been so long since I had felt her lips anywhere on my body, and the simple touch of her lips and tongue upon my fingers was enough to have me ready to rub one off in a public bathroom. I fought the urge and tidied up the mess that the tip of her tongue had caused between my thighs. After washing my hands and dabbing my face with a cool, damp paper towel, I made my way back to my seat in the dark theater.

"You good?" she asked once I sat down.

"Just peachy," I answered, taking a long swallow of my soda.

I tried to refocus on the movie, but it proved to be impossible with this woman sitting right next to me. I already knew it was going to be a 'silver bullet' night for me. *Damn!*

Damn her for being able to turn me on without really trying.

Damn her for sitting there looking completely unaffected by the exchange between us.

Damn her for being so damn sexy!

Damn! Damn! Damn!

Was she really unaware of how she affected me? Did she really have no idea of how just her presence was enough to drive me to distraction? Could she really be that impervious?

I made it through the rest of the movie, though I couldn't begin to tell anyone what took place in it. I was quiet on the ride to the Italian restaurant that she took me to. I quietly exchanged a few texts with Deniece to make sure she and Kayla were okay and then looked out of the window for the rest of the ride.

Before getting out of the car, J.B. asked me if I was okay.

"I'm good," I answered quickly.

"Are you sure?" she asked. "You just got quiet on me all of a sudden."

"I'm sorry. I didn't even realize it," I lied.

I'm horny as hell, and it's all your fault! I wanted to yell at her, but I kept my cool.

She eyed me for a moment before finally opening her door. I

followed suit, stepping out of the car before she could get to my door.

I had to get a hold of myself. I mentally scolded myself and got my little attitude in check before I ruined a perfectly nice evening out with J.B. Once we were seated, I smiled at her.

"Thank you for getting me out of the house tonight."

"It's my pleasure, baby girl," she replied with a smile. "I know you needed a night out. I was actually calling to invite you out earlier, but Deniece beat me to the punch."

I laughed. "Yeah, Deniece is something else."

"I can tell she cares a lot about you. Have you two, um…?"

"No!" I said emphatically. "Hell no! Are you nuts?"

She laughed. "I was just kidding!"

"Don't play like that," I said, putting my hand over my heart in mock terror. "You almost gave me a heart attack!"

She continued to laugh for a minute. "I thought it was funny."

"Hardy-har-har!" I tossed at her sarcastically. "Besides, she is sooo not my type," I joked.

"Is that right?" she asked with a raised eyebrow. "So you've figured out what your type is?" she challenged.

"I've learned," I countered, looking directly into her eyes.

She opened her mouth to speak, but our waiter came to our table. After taking our order, he took our menus and quickly walked away. For the next few minutes, we laughed and debated on whether or not he was "family".

After getting our glasses of white zinfandel, we made a toast to finding happiness. I would have to give Kayla formula milk for a little while, but I wanted to enjoy having a couple of glasses of wine with J.B.

"So," J.B. began after our toast, "what makes you happy?"

"Kayla," I answered automatically.

"What else?" she asked, looking at me intently.

After thinking for a moment, I answered, "Making others

happy. Helping people."

She sat back in her seat and stared at me for a minute. "Okay. Well, when you're not with Kayla or trying to save the world, what brings you pleasure?"

"Pleasure?" I repeated.

"Yes...pleasure."

The tone in her voice made me look her in her eyes. The look she was giving me was laced with mischief. I felt this conversation taking a turn. I cleared my throat and took a sip of my wine.

"Is it too hard of a question?" she taunted. "How about this: when was the last time you experienced pleasure? Not pleasure from being mommy or community service or any of that. When was the last time you received pleasure that was all about *you*?"

The last time we were together, I thought.

"I don't know," I responded instead, unable to look her in the eye anymore.

I was grateful when the waiter arrived with our entrees. I looked down at my food to keep from having to look at her. She, on the other hand, ignored her plate completely after thanking the waiter.

I could feel her eyes on me.

"Nelle," she said in a voice barely above a whisper, though I heard her clearly. "Look at me."

After a moment of hesitancy, I did as she softly commanded.

"Can I please you tonight?"

It took all of my willpower to keep my composure.

"Pardon me?" I said in total surprise.

"Look, I didn't want to come at you wrong, but I've wanted to touch you ever since you opened your door tonight."

The butterflies kicked in, doing double time. My heart was racing all over again, and it felt like my clitoris had a heartbeat.

"J.B., why are you doing this?"

"Because I want you," she answered.

I saw the sincerity in her eyes. I couldn't handle it. I quickly rose and excused myself from the table.

I hurried to the small ladies' room to give myself a moment to gather my wits. I wasn't granted the time. Moments later, J.B. came through the door hot on my tail. After taking in our environment and seeing that we were alone, she locked the door and gently pushed me up against the wall.

I didn't push her away as she brought her body closer to mine. I didn't object when her lips descended onto my own. I opened my mouth and welcomed her tongue as I wrapped my arms around her neck. I pulled her closer to me. I had craved this kiss for over a year and was not going to deny myself what she offered.

Our contact quickly went from sweet and gentle to insistent and wanton. We drank greedily from each other's lips. In a move that both surprised and delighted me, she lifted me off of my feet and sat me on the counter between the twin sinks. She deftly slid the hem of my dress to my waist. Her apt fingers slid under the thin fabric of my thong and easily found their way into my wetness.

"Oh my God," she hissed against my neck. "I've missed this so much."

I could only moan in response as her fingers stroked my drenched clit before sliding into my slippery cavern.

"J.B.!" I cried out, gripping her shoulders while her fingers slid in and out of me repetitively.

"Yes, baby, like that," she groaned in approval as I rocked my hips in rhythm with her fingers. "I want you to cum for me, baby girl."

The demand alone was almost enough to send me over the edge.

"I'm almost there," I moaned in her ear, my sanity slipping with every stroke of her hand.

"Almost ain't good enough," she said, changing the angle of her fingers to touch the sensitive flesh inside of my womb as her thumb stroked my clit. "Cum for me, baby girl!"

"Oh shit," I almost yelled into the crook of her neck as my body gave into her command.

My sanity was gone as I came all over her fingers. My essence flowed from my center onto her hand, and she continued to stroke me deeply, sending me into another orgasmic fit as she sucked on my bottom lip. I moaned as she slid her tongue into the deep recesses of my mouth. My body quaked as she held me with one arm while playing in my womanhood.

Had it not been for the sound of someone trying to come into the bathroom, I don't think she would've stopped. Honestly, I wouldn't have cared.

"Just a minute," she yelled into the air so the person on the other side of the door wouldn't keep trying to open it. Her breathing was as labored as my own. She kissed me deeply before speaking again. "Spend the night with me."

It wasn't a request. It was a command, and a response wasn't necessary.

*****

The ride back to her place was a complete blur. I couldn't remember if we stopped at any traffic lights, or if we listened to music, or if we even talked on the way. I couldn't remember getting there, or going inside, or even if we turned on any lights.

None of it even mattered when she kissed me. The small details ceased to exist as she undressed me. Her fingers and lips caressed my bare skin as my clothing hit the floor. When she brought her lips back to mine, I was in heaven. I held her close, and her hands roamed over my flesh.

I removed her clothes until she wore nothing but her sports bra and underwear. To my delight, she continued to undress. It had been so long that I wasn't sure what to expect anymore.

She pulled me closer to her bare body and whispered, "I don't want anything between us."

We fell to the bed in a flurry of kisses and caresses.

We became science. We fused together and absorbed the quintessence of one another. She became me as I became her. We were one. Entangled. Unified.

We tangoed upon her sheets, a mass of arms and legs. Moans and sighs of pleasure filled the air as we touched one another and drank from each other's fountains. She felt and tasted better than I remembered. For each time her tongue touched my body, mine touched hers. I was in awe as she let me devour her, sip on her nipples, and touch her in ways I never had before. I experienced what it felt like to have her sugar walls constrict around my fingers as she came.

I got high from the magnitude of our lovemaking. We took our time reacquainting our bodies with each other. I memorized every inch of her flesh as we touched and teased each other. Before the night was over, she had donned her apparatus and dove into my wetness, marking my punani all over again.

"Is it still mine, baby?" she asked while slowly pounding into me.

"Always!" I answered in rapture.

"I like that." Her strokes got deeper and harder. "Always, baby?"

"Yes!" I cried out. "Always! Always!"

Her strokes got faster. She started to fuck me hard, and I loved it. She emphasized every stroke with a word. "Is... this... my... pussy?"

"Yes, baby! Yes!"

"Don't you ever give my pussy away again!" she demanded as she beat my femininity to bits and pieces.

"I won't!" I yelled, my nails digging into her shoulders. "Never again! It's yours!"

"Tell me again!"

"It's yours!"

"Again, baby girl!"

"It's yours! It's yours! It's yours!"

We both cried out as we came in unison.

She fell onto my body, gasping for breath as she struggled to recover from such a powerful orgasm. I lay beneath her trying to do the same. After a few minutes, she rolled over and laid next to me. I cuddled up close to her and entwined my legs with hers despite the heat ebbing from both of our bodies. I just wanted her close to me.

She smoothed a damp tendril of hair from my forehead. "Did I hurt you?" she asked quietly. The moonlight streaming through her window highlighted the concern etched on her face.

"I'll definitely feel it in the morning," I answered honestly. "But, it felt so damn good."

The worried look slowly eased from her face. "Do you have any idea how long I've been wanting to make love to you?" she asked.

"Really?" I asked shyly. "All of this time, I've been afraid it was one-sided."

"Not even by a long shot," she replied.

"Are you satisfied now?" I asked nervously. I didn't want this to be a one-night thing, but I didn't want to assume it wasn't.

"I don't think I could ever get enough of you," she answered, looking me in my eyes. "I've missed you, baby girl."

I released a breath of relief. "I've missed you, too, J.B.," I said back, feeling my throat tighten up with emotion. I closed my eyes to ward off the tears I felt brimming up.

For a couple of minutes, neither of us said anything. Finally, I broke the silence with a confession.

"I used to talk to Jazz just to see how you were doing."

She shocked me with her response. "I know."

At the sound of my surprised gasp, she explained, "We almost fell out about it. But, she's how I found out you were pregnant." After a moment of quiet, she asked, "Were you and Travis messing around while we were together?"

"No!" I said, quickly sitting up. "When we were together, no one else mattered. Travis was my friend, and I turned to him hoping it would help me get over losing you."

"Did it work?" she asked calmly.

"No," I answered, looking down at her. "I never got over you."

She pulled me back down into the cradle of her arms so we could 'spoon'.

"Tonight marks a year since I let you walk out of my life," she informed me solemnly.

Has it only been a year?

"I shouldn't have ever let you go," she continued.

"It hurt," I told her honestly. "We both hurt. But, I was blessed with Kayla, so I can't be mad."

"I understand that," she whispered.

"But," I continued, "don't think for one minute there wasn't a day that went by that I didn't think about you."

"I love you, Nelle," she said suddenly. "I want us to try again."

My heart beat faster. "Really?" I asked, turning to face her.

"Do you still love me?" she asked. Uncertainty flashed in her eyes.

"I never stopped," I confessed.

"Tell me then."

"I love you, J.B. I always have."

"Can we try again?" she asked. "Will you be my lady?"

"Yes."

Chapter 27
Heaven & Hell

J.B.

Heaven on Earth.

That is where I was at that point in my life. She was back in my life. She was my lady again. I couldn't be happier. I had the woman I loved and her daughter in my life. I felt complete. The days seemed brighter. I felt passion in my life again.

I couldn't begin to guess how often we made love. The distance that had been between us since before her pregnancy fueled our hunger for each other. We were insatiable. When I wasn't on campus, I was with her. When we weren't making love, we were together fighting the urge to do so. Even when we fed or played with Kayla, there was electricity in the air. I was grateful the baby wasn't old enough to sit up on her own. She would've definitely learned some new and unusual things during the late night hours.

A majority of our nights were spent touching and teasing, then talking until we fell asleep. I virtually lived with her. I had a drawer in her bedroom and a toothbrush for me had returned to her bathroom. Even Travis had gotten used to seeing me!

I knew he still had a little resentment towards me, but it didn't bother me. I could understand why he had an issue with me. I knew it had to be a blow to his ego for the woman who gave him a child to be in love with me. As I got used to him, I almost felt bad for him. However, there was no way in hell I felt bad enough to let her go.

This woman had me heart and soul, and I had her. After what we had been through, I was sure it would be smooth sailing from that point on.

Boy, was I wrong.

In hindsight, I should've known better. When Nelle told me that her mother had invited us to her church's Easter program and dinner, I instinctively wanted to say no. However, she had been so excited about the "breakthrough" that I didn't want to rain on her parade.

The first issue was the church and their response to Shanelle and me coming in together. I was already prepared for the gasps, looks of surprise, and the whispers that slowly made their way around the church. Nelle, on the other hand, was not quite as ready. She tried to keep a strong front up as we walked into the building with me holding her daughter as if she was my own, but after we took our seats on the same row as her parents, she never even glanced my way, keeping her attention on Kayla as the reverend preached about the Resurrection.

After the service, we waited for her parents outside. I could feel several sets of eyes on us as we baked under the bright sun.

"Are you okay?" I said to Shanelle as we made our way towards a patch of shade to protect Kayla's skin.

"Yeah," she answered. "I just have this feeling I've never had before. I grew up going to this church, and for the first time ever, I wasn't at ease being here."

"Is it because of me?" I asked.

"No," she answered quickly.

"Are you sure?" I pressed, but she was saved from answering when her mother walked up to us.

"I hope you enjoyed the service," Mrs. Carter said to me with a voice laced in saccharine.

"It was nice," I answered with just as much synthetic sugar. "Thank you for the invitation."

"Of course," she answered, then turned her attention to Nelle. "Reverend Clay will be joining us for dinner," she said while playing with Kayla's balled up fingers. "We will meet you at the house."

It was my first time at her parents' house, and for a split second, I thought I was on the set of *The Fresh Prince of Bel-Air*. I waited to see if Geoffrey was going to walk in with Will Smith.

So this is how the 'silver spoon' class lives, I thought to myself as we went into the den to make ourselves more comfortable. Not that I was in awe over their trappings, because my family was doing pretty good for themselves, as well. It was just that the Carters seemed a little over the top in my opinion. From what Nelle had told me, her mother, Diana, was raised in a small town and had a down-to-earth family. I wondered what had caused her to become so pompous. Once it was announced that dinner was almost ready, I wondered when the last time was that Mrs. Carter had cooked a meal for husband. Had she ever?

As I watched Mr. Carter pad through the house, it was apparent he was cared for and respected by the people who worked in their home. He had a quiet demeanor, but I knew of his business savvy and knew he could be a shark when he needed to be. Dale Carter, the businessman, was a completely different person from Dale Carter, the husband and father. He seemed perfectly content with letting his wife and daughter have their way as long as he had his peace. He was never rude to me, and I never got any negative vibes from him. So, I couldn't knock him. I couldn't help but wonder what had made him fall in love with Diana. True, she was beautiful, even in her later years, but what more was it to make him want to wife her up. Maybe she had some good pussy. Lawd knows her daughter did.

I chuckled to myself at the thought.

"What's so funny?" Shanelle asked, drawing me out of my reverie.

"Nothin', baby girl," I answered, actually feeling my face get warm. Then I leaned over and whispered in her ear, "I was just thinking about your body."

I saw her blush and fell deeper in love. Even after all of this time, I could still make her bashful, and I hoped it would never change.

"Excuse me," her mother said abruptly, noticing our exchange. She walked over and gently took Kayla out of Nelle's arms. "I will go lay her down in the nursery so we can eat. The reverend is here, and dinner is ready."

Once we were all seated, the reverend said grace. It went downhill from there.

"So," her mother began, "tell us a little about yourself, J.B."

"Well, I come from a family of…"

Yadda-yadda-yadda, blah-blah-blah. This was the easy part, but then it finally came.

The bullshit.

"And how long have you known our Shanelle?"

This question came from the reverend.

"Well, we both attend school together," I answered. "We've been close for almost two years now."

"So you're pretty good friends, huh?" he asked, curious.

"Yes, we are," I answered carefully, then waited for it.

"How good?" he answered, looking me directly in my eyes.

"Personally, sir," I responded. "I'm not sure why it's of any importance to you."

The reverend wiped his mouth and kept looking at me. "I'm going to be honest with you. There was a lot of talk going on about you and our Shanelle amongst my congregation today."

"Then maybe you should be addressing your congregation about gossip in your next sermon, Reverend," I said coolly.

For a moment, he was taken aback, but he continued. "Shanelle has always been a good girl. Comes from a loving family. She was raised right."

"And so was I," I informed him.

"I don't know you from a can of paint—" he began, but I cut him off.

"You are absolutely correct," I told him. "You know absolutely nothing about me."

"Well, I know you being here is proof that you are clouding that poor girl's judgment—"

"There is nothing wrong with my judgment," Nelle jumped in, standing up.

"Shanelle, you stay out of this," Mrs. Carter scolded. "This is between your friend and the reverend."

"Shanelle, you don't know what you're doing," the reverend said to her. "I know this may seem like fun now, but this is not the way of the bible. You were raised better than *this*."

"Better than what?" I demanded, standing up, as well. It took everything in me to keep from telling this man to go and fuck himself.

"You have this poor child thinking she loves you," he said.

"I'm a grown woman," Shanelle yelled, "and my love for J.B. is genuine!"

"See what you've caused," he said to me. "She has never been disrespectful, and look at her now."

"She's not being disrespectful," I countered. "She's defending herself. Y'all are on some other shit. I knew when Nelle told me about this invitation that there was gonna be some bullshit involved. Bringing a reverend into Shanelle's personal business? Really?"

The look her mother gave me was one of distaste.

"Rude," she said. Then she looked at Shanelle. "Is this what you really want? Someone who will come into your home and disrespect your family? To have members of your church snicker and talk behind your back? To have strangers look at you with disgust?"

"It seems like the only ones who are doing it are you all," Nelle replied. "I'm sorry if my choices are such a problem for you, but they are *my* choices. I love J.B., and *she* is what I want. If you can't handle that, then we shouldn't even be here." She stepped around her seat. "J.B., I'm ready to go."

"You ain't said nothin', baby," I told her. "I was ready to go when I got here."

She went and got Kayla from the nursery, and we headed back to her place.

After bathing and feeding Kayla, she laid her down to sleep. Then we laid down, also, and I let her cry in my arms until she fell asleep.

I was pissed. I had already gone through some of the judgmental and ignorant shit that my love was experiencing. But, I didn't have the extra hurt of having it all come at the hands of my mother. That was some cold and calculating shit she had pulled. True, my family wasn't happy about it when I came out, but they eventually got over it. So, I guess I was just more fortunate.

I didn't know what I could do to ease her pain. I wanted nothing more than to let her know how much I loved her and that as long as she had me, she would never be alone. She was loved completely. She always had been.

Would it be wrong of me to say she didn't need her family as long as she had me? Possibly, but that is how I felt. In my personal opinion, her mother was a bitch who couldn't get over herself. And her dad…I didn't know what to say about him. What man lets another man talk to his child any kind of way and say nothing? I lost a lot of respect for him in that moment.

Imagine my surprise when there was a knock on her front door and it turned out to be him.

"Can I come in?" he asked, looking solemn.

I stepped aside to allow him entry. After all, he was her father, and this was her place.

"Shanelle is asleep," I informed him.

"That's fine," he said. "I came to see you."

"Me?" I asked, surprised.

"Yes," he answered. "After an evening like tonight, I was sure you would be here with her."

"I'm always here for her," I told him as I took a seat on the sofa. He sat on the opposite end.

"I wanted to apologize to you for how my wife acted with you," he began. "Sometimes she's overdramatic."

"The thing is, sir, she's not hurting me. She's hurting Nelle."

"I know this," he replied. "When we first found out about you and my daughter, I wasn't happy about it at all. I always pictured myself walking her down the aisle and presenting her to a young man. I never thought I would see the day that my daughter would be in love with another woman. But, she loves you. I can tell. I just want my baby to be happy. I thought Diane would snap out of it, but tonight showed me that she hasn't. We had an argument about it tonight. I don't know what's going to happen between the two of them."

"One thing I do know," I told him, "is if she keeps it up, she is going to mess around and lose Nelle and Kayla completely."

After a moment of silence, I spoke again. "I love your daughter. No one is going to love her more or treat her better than I will. I will bet my life on that."

After looking at me for a moment, he said, "I believe you."

We talked for a few more minutes before he peeked in on Nelle and Kayla and then left. I felt better about him, but I knew dealing with his wife was going to be a whole other ordeal. I knew it would only be a matter of time before I ended up going off on her, but I would try to keep my cool for Shanelle's sake.

As I laid back down with her and felt her adjust to be closer to me, I knew there was only one thing left for me to do.

*****

One morning a few days later, as she sat up in her bed, I brought a tray with a covered breakfast consisting of scrambled eggs, bacon, buttered toast, jelly, orange juice, and a flawless solitaire on a simple gold band in a velvet box.

As she looked at me with surprise written all over her face, I removed the ring from the box and slid it onto her ring finger.

"I don't have any suave words to say," I began, "so I will just keep it simple. Will you marry me?"

"Simple works for me," she said with a smile. Her response was also simple, and with one word she sealed the deal. "Yes."

Then all was right in my world.

Chapter 28
Found

Shanelle

The set-up was beautiful. The colors were pink and white. White and pink flowers and ribbons were everywhere in the small church. It was a beautiful day. The sun beamed and easily surpassed the stained glass windows of the chapel. It was the perfect day for a wedding.

I smiled at J.B., and she smiled back at me.

I then looked over at my father who happily held Kayla in his lap. He seemed to be the only person who could keep her absolutely still without a fight. At eighteen months of age, she was a very active little girl, and she was a major Grandpa's baby.

I then looked over at Deniece, my best friend. We glanced at each other with tears of joy in our eyes. It was such a joyous occasion, and I was so glad we could share it. I felt so privileged to be her maid of honor.

"I now pronounce you husband and wife. You may now kiss your bride."

Fresh out of college, she ended up getting engaged to a young man who she had been seeing off and on while we were in school. She was happy, and I was happy for her.

It was their wedding day. I held her bouquet as she kissed her husband for the first time. A tear slipped from my eye as I watched the joyful scene.

"I am pleased to present to you all, Mr. and Mrs. William Hughs."

I applauded with the rest of the guests while the music played in the background.

As we exchanged hugs, she whispered in my ear, "It's your turn now."

I could only smile. She was right. In a couple of months to follow, J.B. and I would be exchanging our vows, as well.

When she proposed to me, I had quickly said yes, but I wanted us to take our time. There had still been hurdles to cross, and I wanted to make sure everything was right, because I only planned to do this ceremony thing once.

Things are not always easy with us, but we make it work. We have our disagreements and even our arguments, but that is to be expected when two women are in a relationship. At least, I think so.

In almost two years, my mother still hadn't come around, but I refused to sacrifice my happiness and a love of my own just to make her happy. If she ever wanted to come around, she knew the address where J.B. and I lived. I had extended an olive branch through my father, and that was as far as I was willing to go. I loved my mother, but I had my own family now.

The bond between J.B. and I was as strong as steel. She made me feel safe, valued, and loved. She still gave me butterflies with just a look, and she set my body on fire with a touch.

Sometimes I wondered where I would be if she had not come into my life. Would I have ended up with Travis? Would I have met someone else who could've made me feel the same way? Somehow, I doubt it. I think back to where we began, and I am so grateful for how she helped me grow and discover who I am. She was more than just my partner. She was my soul's mate. I believe she had been created just for me, to love me and to *teach me* how to love.

There were still times when I wondered if I needed a label. Every blue moon, there were still guys that I saw and found attractive. There were definitely women that I found attractive. But, in all honesty, nobody can take the place of the woman that I love.

I am simply the woman who fell in love with the person who I was meant to be with. When I found Jocelyn Brianna Donovan, she helped me find...me.

*****

J.B.

I don't know if there are words that can fully express the state of bliss that I've been in since Nelle said yes to my proposal. Times have not always been perfect. As a matter of fact, we've had our fair share of drama, major and minor.

I've had to watch Nelle's frustration with finishing school, working while trying not to depend on her trust fund, and her dealings with her mother. She has tried to keep a brave face on for me when it comes to her mother, but I know it hurts her that her mother is so difficult when it comes to us. On a brighter side, my mother is definitely playing her part as a doting grandmother and future mother-in-law, and seems thrilled that Nelle will soon be a part of our family. It makes me happy to know that Nelle will still get the unconditional love and affection that a mother gives a daughter from *mine*. Sometimes, it happens that way, though.

I take my responsibility as her mate seriously. I take joy in knowing that I am her rock, her shoulder, and soon, her life partner. It was a bumpy ride, but it was so worth it. I had to learn patience and understanding. I'm so glad I finally did. I still have my moments when my patience is tested. Nelle knows what buttons to push to work my nerves. She also knows what it takes to soothe me.

It has been a beautiful experience watching her become her own woman. *My* woman. She stands beside me proudly and is learning not to worry about what others may think about her or us.

She is my queen, and she says I am her knight in shining armor. Kayla is our princess, and we are a happy family.

I dare say that Travis and I have even become friends. He finally moved on and has a girlfriend, but sometimes I still catch those occasional wistful glances when we are all in the same room. I can't blame him. My Nelle is one hell of a woman, so I can't fault him for still having feelings for her. After all, I was in his shoes at a point in time.

Each morning, I wake up and look at the woman that I love and the little girl that I've claimed as my own, and I am grateful for all that I have. It amazes me that it all started with a glance.

A glance that led to a conversation, which led to a date, which led me to a journey where I found the greatest thing that I could ever find...the love of my life. I experienced finding love, bliss, pleasure, anger, heartache, growth, and finding love all over again. I would do it all over again as long as I ended up exactly where I was meant to be...with my woman.

I don't know whether I found her or if she found me, but I know that in the near future, we can both be found exchanging our vows and letting the world know we are in love and we are going to make good shit happen for *our* family. That's all that matters to me.

What else needs to be said?

About the Author

Renee has been featured in two erotic anthologies. *She Say, She Say* is her debut romance novel and the first of many works of literature to come. She believes fiction can be romantic, steamy, and true-to-life.

Coinciding with her passion for writing is her passion for hair and hair care. She is training to obtain her certification in Cosmetology through the world renowned John Paul Mitchell Systems, a leader in the industry.

A self-proclaimed big kid and country girl, she enjoys spending as much time playing computer games as she does going fishing, both hobbies that she shares with her two daughters. She currently resides in North Little Rock, Arkansas, but says that "Anywhere" in Georgia is home.

Made in the USA
Middletown, DE
29 March 2015